THE CHRISTMAS EXCHANGE

CALI MELLE

For everyone who made the naughty list this year...
May your holiday be merry and smutty.

CHAPTER ONE

As the cab pulled up in front of my parents' old colonial home, I paused just inside the vehicle for a moment. They weren't expecting me until later this evening, but I ended up switching to an earlier flight and got in a few hours before my mother was supposed to pick me up from the airport. My movements were unhurried as I slowly climbed out of my seat and stepped out onto the sidewalk.

I tipped the driver as he handed me my bag and I stood on the curb, staring up at the house for a moment. Inhaling deeply, I sucked the clean, crisp mountain air into my lungs and closed my eyes. It had been almost an entire year since I had come back to my hometown. I would be lying if I said there wasn't a part of me that didn't miss this place.

Almost ten years ago I left for college in New York

City, and I never looked back. The city was where I truly belonged, but there was something about the mountains that always called me back. I enjoyed the constant movement where I lived. Time moved in fast-forward, never slowing. Every now and then, it was nice to take a step back and breathe in the fresh air while staring up at the open skies that weren't obscured by skyscrapers.

There was a part of me that was a little anxious about being back in my hometown. It had been a few years since I last saw my best friends whom I grew up with. We had all grown apart over the years, even though we had tried to stay in contact. I wasn't sure if they would be back in town for the holiday or not, but I was hoping I'd see them at some point. At the same time, I was a little nervous about the possibility of running into them again.

So much time had passed, I was afraid so much would have changed.

Opening my eyes, I stared back at the house that loomed above me. I always swore this place was haunted when I was a kid, but as my eyes trailed over the Christmas lights hanging from the gutters, I found it hard to believe. It looked like the North Pole had thrown up all over the exterior of the house. My mother's style was always softer and delicate, but she didn't hold back when it came to Christmas.

Grabbing my suitcase, I stepped up to the front gate and opened it before stepping into the front yard. The wheels of my suitcase moved over the concrete walkway as I dodged small clumps of snow until I reached the front steps. Hoisting it up, I walked across the front porch that wrapped around the house. My hand touched the cool metal handle of the front door and I pushed it down before letting myself in.

It was warm and welcoming inside, a stark contrast to the cold winter air outside. The smell of vanilla and cinnamon enveloped me, drawing me deeper into the house. The sound of my mother's voice as she hummed drifted down the hall and I left my suitcase in the foyer by the stairs before stepping into the kitchen. She was moving around the island when she caught sight of me.

A gasp escaped her and she jumped, lifting her hand to her chest. "Oh my goodness, Raegan! You scared me." She paused, her eyebrows scrunching before glancing at the clock on the stove. "Wait. Raegan? I'm supposed to pick you up from the airport after dinner."

I shrugged off my long wool coat and smiled brightly at my mother. "I was able to get an earlier flight and thought I would come early and surprise you."

Her lips stretched into a grin and she rounded the island before pulling me in for a hug. "And what a pleasant surprise this is! I'm so happy you're here, dear." She pulled away, smoothing the arms of my sage green sweater. "How was your flight?"

"It wasn't terrible," I told her, watching her as she moved over to the counter to pour me a cup of coffee.

Steam drifted from the top of the mug as she poured some caramel-flavored creamer into it before handing it to me. "I was able to get some work done on the flight, so it helped to pass the time."

I worked for one of the top marketing firms in the city and oversaw various projects for some of the biggest retail companies in the world. It was a time-consuming job, but lucky for me, I was driven and working my way to the top. My dating life was dismal and I didn't leave much time for other hobbies. I was basically married to my job.

"I'm glad you were able to get the time off to come visit."

I was an only child and I knew it was rough on my mother when I decided to fly from the nest. Especially when I moved so far away. We talked regularly and I tried to come visit when I could, but this past year was just so hectic I couldn't get the time off that I wanted to. I felt guilty, especially with the sadness in her smile as she looked at me in that moment, but such was life.

I smiled back at her. "Me too."

"Well, since you're home, why don't you take your things to your room and get settled in. I'm sure you're tired from traveling. I have to head to the market in a bit to get some things for Christmas dinner."

I tilted my head to the side. "I'm actually not that tired. Perhaps I could join you?"

Her face lit up. "I would love that."

"Perfect."

––––––

After taking my stuff up to my old bedroom, my mother and I headed into town to go to Finnegan's Market. It was a large warehouse that was set up with various stands, along with a small grocery store in the center. It was where most people in the town frequented to do any shopping, whether it was for food or other items. The only thing they didn't have was clothing, but if you were looking for small knick knacks, you could find it all there.

My mother and I parted ways as she stepped into the grocery store to do her shopping and I made my way around, checking out the different stands. I had brought my parents gifts back from New York, so there wasn't a need to buy anything here, but I couldn't resist looking at the handcrafted things you could find only at Finnegan's.

Mr. Murray had his usual stand set up with his sculptured wooden animals. Everything he made was from wood he cut down from the forest on his property and he hand-carved every single piece. I was looking at the resin cutting boards he had added to his inventory when I heard my name.

"Raegan Thompson!" The voice was deep as it rumbled from his chest. A voice I would have known anywhere. I spun around and saw Miles striding toward me.

He was one of my closest friends growing up. His

parents and my parents were friends and we were literally inseparable. That was until we both left for college and moved away from Delmont Ridge. His sandy brown hair was a perfect mess on top of his head and his blue eyes met mine as he stopped directly in front of me.

The navy sweater he was wearing hugged his muscles and I allowed my eyes one opportunity to scan his physique, but only for a brief moment. If I allowed my eyes to linger any longer, it would only ignite the old feelings I used to have for him. Feelings I always kept to myself because he was one of my best friends. Being attracted to him would have never ended well— plus, he was always dating different girls.

"Well, if it isn't Miles Walker. What are you doing here?"

A smirk pulled on his lips. "Home for the holidays. My mother said yours told her you'd be back in town. I planned on hunting you down, but you just made my job easier."

A soft laugh escaped me and I shook my head at him. "How have you been? It's been far too long."

"You're telling me." He chuckled. "We really need to make it a habit to meet up more than just when we're both back home. I'm fairly certain we only live about an hour away from each other. You're still in Manhattan, right?"

I nodded. "You're in Jersey, just over the bridge?"

Miles nodded. "I will say, I'm not a fan of the city,

but I'd deal with the lunatics on the road if it meant I got to see you."

"Yeah, well, we'll have to see about making that happen then, won't we?"

His eyes were unreadable for a moment as he stared down at me, deep into my hazel eyes. Given he was at least a foot taller, I always had to tip my head back to be able to meet his gaze. "What are you doing tonight?" He paused for a moment, his tongue darting out to wet his lips. "I mean, we are both back in town, so why wait until we're back on the East Coast to hang out?"

I mulled over his words. My mother didn't say anything about any plans. From what I knew, we didn't have anything officially planned until Christmas Day. "What did you have in mind?"

"Julian and I are meeting at The Swan around eight. Want to meet us there?"

My breath caught in my throat at the mention of his name, surprised to hear he was back for the holidays as well. Julian Foster. The third leg to our trio. The three of us were inseparable while we were growing up, until we graduated from high school. Julian had us beat in terms of moving far away from Delmont Ridge. He moved to an entirely different country and spent his days in the beautiful city of Venice.

I had gone to visit him once, three years ago... but that was a different story.

One I would never share with the world.

7

"Sure, I'll be there," I told him as my mother walked up to me. She stepped up to the two of us with a smile.

"Hi, Miles," she said softly, and he grinned at her as he pulled her in for a hug. "Your mother said you'd be coming home for Christmas, but I didn't expect to see you here."

Miles lifted his grocery bag and smiled sheepishly. "Just picking a few things up for the feast. It was nice seeing you," he said to my mother before turning to me. "I'll see you this evening."

"See you on Christmas, Miles," my mother said with a nod, and Miles winked at me before disappearing into the crowd. I was a little confused by her response to him. Why would she see him on Christmas Day?

I turned to look at my mother with a scowl. "Why are you going to see him on Christmas?"

My mother gave me a knowing look. "I thought I told you the plans for this year, Raegan. Eleanor, Laura, and I all decided we would get together with our families, like we used to before you guys all left for college. We're going to celebrate the holiday with the Walkers and the Fosters."

CHAPTER TWO

Main Street in Delmont Ridge was busy by the time I was there trying to find a parking spot. Living in a small town meant all of the locals were usually out around this time of year. There were different traditions, between the lighting of the town Christmas tree, caroling, Santa being at the local fire hall, among other events. There was always something going on and as it got closer to the actual holiday, many people were rushing to stores to get last-minute gifts or out for a drink to unwind from the hustle and bustle of the season.

I was able to secure the last parking spot in The Swan's lot. There were only a few spots I had passed on the street, but thankfully I was able to get the last one in the actual parking lot. After leaving my mother's car, I trudged through remnants of the last snowstorm on the ground. A light flurry of snowflakes was falling from the sky as I made my way to the entrance of the bar.

As I stepped inside, I was greeted with loud Christmas tunes playing from the jukebox in the back corner. The Swan was a total dive bar and it was the local watering hole here. It was like stepping back in time, walking inside. Delmont Ridge always felt like it was moving years behind the rest of the world. It was weirdly therapeutic and gave a sense of nostalgia.

It was a stark contrast to what I had grown used to living in New York City. I welcomed taking a step back. A few heads turned to the door as I walked inside and brushed the snow from my peacoat. Familiar faces lifted their hands in greeting or said hello as I walked past them. One nice thing about Delmont Ridge, they followed the rest of the world with banning smoking indoors.

I was grateful for that progressive movement on their part.

It was a quaint little town. Everyone knew everyone. Which also came with the annoyance of nosy people and everyone knowing each other's business. I did enjoy it, though. The familiarity of it all. It brought an overwhelming sense of calm and peace. Like I had a place here, even though I was detached from this world.

As I rounded the corner of the bar, I spotted Miles sitting in one of the booths. He was facing me, his eyes lighting up when he saw me. Julian was sitting facing him, his back to me. He had a beanie pulled over his inky black hair, but small tendrils poked from beneath the material.

Miles rose to his feet as I walked over to their table while I shrugged out of my coat. A smile was on his lips and he pulled me in for a hug. Closing my eyes, I inhaled his scent—cedar and moss. His body was solid and warm against mine, his arms holding me close for a moment longer than I expected. "I'm so glad you came." He smiled at me as he pulled away.

Much to my surprise, Julian was also on his feet. I moved away from Miles and turned to face Julian. His dark brown, almost midnight eyes met mine. The corners of his lips twitched. "Raegan," he spoke my name slowly and softly. His voice was hoarse and his throat bobbed as he swallowed roughly. "It's good to see you."

He closed the distance between us and wrapped his large arms around me. His hands were splayed out against my back and I could feel his warmth through the layer of my sweater. His scent drifted into my nose and I allowed myself one breath of him. He smelled earthy—like sandalwood—with a mixture of pure mountain air.

We broke apart after a minute and Miles stepped up to me, wrapping his arm around mine. "Come sit," he urged, pulling me toward the booth with him. Julian slid back into his seat and I followed after Miles, sitting beside him. "Did you want some beer? We just ordered a fresh pitcher."

I wasn't much of a beer drinker, but I agreed with a smile and a nod. "I'll drink whatever you two are drinking."

Julian was silent, as per usual, just watching Miles and me as we were the only two speaking. They were almost polar opposites, the perfect yin and yang. Miles was more of an extrovert and the life of the party. Julian was quiet. He sat back and observed the world moving around him. They coexisted perfectly together.

And not to mention both of them had always been nice to look at. They had both aged like fine wine as the three of us were approaching our thirties. More mature, filled out, and manly. They had a way of making my breath catch in my throat as my mouth went drier than the damn desert.

But then again... they both seemed to always have that effect on me.

One of the bartenders called Julian over and he left the table for a moment to grab the pitcher and another glass. Miles turned to me, his bright blue eyes meeting mine.

"So, how have you been, Rae? What's new in your life?"

I shrugged as Julian came back to us and filled both of their mugs before handing me one. "I've been good. Just really busy with work. There isn't honestly anything new. I've had a few projects I've been working on that have taken up a lot of my time."

Miles cocked his head to the side as mischief danced across his face. "How's the dating scene in the city?"

I snorted, almost spitting out my beer. "That's a better suited question for someone who's actually in the scene. I'm not dating anymore, nor do I have any plans to do so anytime soon."

"Why?"

Julian's voice took me by surprise and I turned to look over at him. His dark eyes were trained on me, giving absolutely nothing away.

"I don't really have time to date right now. I don't need the added distractions and, honestly, after the few dates I did go on, I've discovered there aren't as many fish in the ocean as you'd think." I paused and looked between them. "Okay, it's both of your turn now. Enough about me."

I turned to Miles as Julian simply lifted his mug and took a sip of his beer, not offering to be the one who went first.

"Can't complain about anything," Miles replied with a shrug. "I've also been keeping myself busy with work and have to agree with dating. Maybe I'm just picky, but I haven't found anyone worth my time or interest." He glanced at Julian. "What about you? How's your glorious life abroad?"

"It's fine," he said with indifference. "I'm considering moving back to the States."

My eyes widened and I stared at him for a moment. "I thought you loved Italy."

"Oh, I do. I think it's time for me to move on, though. I've been there for a considerable amount of time now."

I was honestly shocked by it. Julian didn't speak much about it, but he was living the dream over there in the beautiful city he lived in. It had been some time since we last spoke, so maybe there was more to it than I had realized. I was curious, though. It seemed to be out of nowhere, but Julian didn't do things without carefully considering every option and angle.

"So, you just want to move back here because you've been there for so long?" Miles questioned him as he slung his arm over the tops of my shoulders. "Seems strange, if you ask me."

"Is it a crime to miss my family and friends?"

Miles snorted. "You have friends other than the two of us?"

Julian stared blankly at him. "Not really." He directed his gaze to me and there was a slow, steady fire burning in his dark irises. "Unfortunately, the two of you are the only ones who have managed to keep my attention long enough."

My tongue stuck to the roof of my mouth. I lifted my glass of beer to my lips and took a long drink of it. "Where would you move if you came back?"

Julian shrugged. "I haven't decided yet, but when I do, you'll know."

Miles traced invisible patterns on my bicep. His body was warm against mine and I was acutely aware of how close he was to me. I was pressed against his side with his thigh pressed against mine. My mind traced every edge that was touching him. Warmth built in my stomach and I wasn't sure if it was because of how Julian was still looking at me or how my body relaxed against Miles.

They were both bad for my health, which is why I never allowed myself to cross any lines with either of them when we were in high school. That was a partial lie. I did share one drunken kiss with Miles, which I was fairly certain he didn't even remember. Our teenage years were messy for all three of us, trying to figure out where we were headed in life.

I valued their friendships more than anything. They were always protective, making sure I was safe. I was terrified of losing both of them, especially with how long we had been friends. They were deeply embedded into my life, even if we didn't see each other as often now. If I ever uttered a word of being attracted to either one of them, it could have gone terribly. That rejection was something I never wanted to experience. So, the three of us always remained friends.

Even after I went to visit Julian three years ago…

We swore we would never speak of that night again. It was simply a mistake. Another drunken kiss, although neither of us were drunk on alcohol. We were caught up in the moment. In the romantic air of Italy one evening. As quickly as it happened, it ended.

That was the one time I allowed myself to show any

type of attraction to him. I made the mistake of initiating a kiss—one he returned passionately, before he abruptly pulled away from me and told me he had a girlfriend. Things were a touch awkward after that, but we were able to maintain our friendship and pretend like it never happened.

He and his girlfriend broke up about a month later, but even then, it didn't change things between us. Things were the way they were supposed to be between the three of us. And in this moment, it just felt good to be back together again. *Just like old times...*

Miles grabbed his mug and lifted it up as he raised it in the middle of the table. He looked between Julian and me as we both watched him. "Lift your glasses, you idiots. I'm trying to make a toast here."

Julian chuckled and raised his mug, a smile pulling on my lips as I did the same. The three of us held our glasses toward one another.

"To old friends. Reconnecting and making new memories. And to the three of us being back together again." He paused as a grin spread across his lips. "This isn't just a toast, but also a promise that we'll all make more of a conscious effort to be in each other's lives again, regardless of how busy we are. We've been life-long friends, so let's make it last a lifetime."

"To us," I agreed, pressing my glass against his. We both looked to Julian who was just holding his own in the air.

A smirk pulled on his lips and stars danced in his

midnight irises. "To us," he echoed as he pressed his glass to Miles' and mine.

The three of us pulled them away, each of us throwing back some of the hoppy liquid. I looked between the two men, both of their gazes finding mine, and I couldn't help but smile.

It felt good to be back in Delmont Ridge.

But more than anything, it felt good to be back with them.

CHAPTER THREE

I t was still dark outside when I woke up the next
morning. The days were always shorter in the
winter and with the time change from New York
to Colorado, my body still hadn't adjusted. I rolled out
of bed and made my way down to the kitchen, careful
to be quiet so I didn't wake anyone else up. As I
glanced at the clock while popping a pod into the coffee
maker, I noticed it was only five thirty in the morning.

I may have been a natural morning person, but this
was too early for me. I waited patiently for my coffee,
scrolling the different social media apps on my phone.
My laptop was sitting on the kitchen island where I had
left it yesterday and I fought the urge to grab it. I could
easily just open it up and work on a few things while
everyone else was still asleep.

This was the problem I had in life. I never knew
when to just set things to the side. Work was always my

number one priority, but I needed to change that—at least while I was technically on vacation. It was a holiday and I could spare a few days. It wouldn't set me back on any of my deadlines, but had a way of prickling my anxiety instead.

Walking right past my laptop, I headed into the living room and curled up on the couch with my cup of coffee. I continued to mindlessly scroll on my phone before grabbing a paperback book that was sitting on the coffee table in front of me. Lifting it up in front of my face, I scanned the front and back of the fantasy novel before flipping to the first page.

There was a time in my life that I used to be a big reader. I would devour and consume books like my life depended on it. That was before I went to college and immersed myself in a world of work. It felt refreshing to be torn from reality and thrust back into a fictional setting.

"*The Cruel Prince* is one of my recent favorites," my mother's voice sounded from the kitchen, pulling me out of the fantasy world I had lost myself in.

I glanced over at her, my eyes wide as I realized I was sitting on the couch in my parents' house and not lost in Elfhame.

I blinked momentarily. My coffee had since grown cold and two whole hours had passed since I initially walked downstairs.

"I—uh—I found it sitting on the table and figured I could use a distraction."

My mother smiled brightly from where she was standing. "You used to read all the time. I'm just happy to see you so lost in a book instead of your work."

"Yeah, it's been a long time since I've read anything that wasn't work related. It has been a nice escape."

"When did you get up?" my mother asked me as she came over to the living room and sat down on one of the armchairs. "I thought I heard someone moving around earlier."

"It was around five thirty." I shrugged dismissively. "Still adjusting to the time difference."

My mother nodded as a sad smile pulled on her lips. "You know, if you just lived in Delmont Ridge all the time, you'd never have to deal with the time difference."

As she was growing older, my mother desperately wanted me to be closer to home. I couldn't help but feel guilty whenever she brought it up. I could potentially move back and work remotely, but I couldn't help but be afraid of the feeling of being isolated, as if I were trapped.

I loved my hometown, but growing up in a small town had a way of making you feel as if you were suffocating. You just need a change of scenery and pace. Something different from what you've known your entire life. Or, you could be the exception and be the type of person who never moved away.

My mother would have preferred me to be the latter.

"I'm home for the holidays and I really do want to

try to visit more. I promise I will make more of an effort to come here more often."

My mother frowned. "I wouldn't actually expect you to move back home. I just worry about you, Raegan. I don't want to see you burn yourself out. You work so hard, I just worry about whether or not you're actually living your life to the fullest or just going through the motions of it."

I lifted the book in my hand to show it to her. "I'm taking a break right now."

She let out an exasperated sigh. "You know what I mean."

My phone vibrated from where it was sitting on the couch next to me. I lifted it up to read the name that came across with the call. Miles. My forehead creased. It was seven thirty in the morning. What could he possibly need?

"Hello?"

He chuckled softly. "Good morning, sunshine. I wasn't sure if you would be awake yet or not."

"I was wondering why you were awake this early and calling me right now," I told him as my mind drifted back to last night. The three of us ended up staying out until midnight, but it was still a long day of traveling, the time difference, and then throw in some alcohol.

"Technically, it would be nine thirty at home right now." He paused for a moment. "I woke up early and figured you would be awake too since you live on the East Coast."

A soft laugh escaped me. "I've been up since five thirty. My body has no idea what is going on right now."

Miles was silent for a moment and I didn't miss the smile on my mother's lips as she ducked her face to look at her own phone. She had one ear pointed toward me, listening to my conversation, as she made it appear like she was reading something extremely important on her phone.

"So, I have this idea that might be kind of crazy because it's last minute, but I want you to consider it before throwing it out the window completely."

I couldn't help but laugh again. Miles was always the one who had the most random, off-the-wall ideas. And I was always the one who put him in check and told him no. Julian never said much, he just let me handle things and watched the interactions with mischief dancing in his eyes.

"Fine." I smiled and shook my head. "Let's hear your idea, Miles."

"Wait, I'm going to add Julian to the call because I need him to hear it too."

I heard the click through the phone before I had a chance to respond. It wasn't long before Miles connected the three of us on one call.

"Are you both here? Raegan? Julia?"

I snorted. "Yes, I'm here."

Julian was silent for a beat. "Call me that one more time and you won't be able to talk again."

"Okay, perfect," Miles said brightly without even entertaining Julian's grumpiness. "You're both here. So, I was thinking... since we're all home for the holidays and it has literally been years since we've done it, I think it's time we go on another ski trip."

Julian didn't say anything in response.

"Miles, Christmas is in two days. We can't go on a trip right now."

"But we can. We can go up to Opal Peak just for the night. It's only forty-five minutes away, so it's not like we'll be far. We can ski today and tomorrow and then head home." He spoke in such a rush, like he needed to get the words out before someone objected to his idea. "We won't miss Christmas. And remember the promise we made?"

I glanced over at my mother who was all ears and eyes now. I narrowed mine at her and she nodded eagerly. "Go," she mouthed to me. Bless her heart. She just wanted me to live some kind of life that wasn't completely consumed with work.

Julian was still silent. There was a part of me that wondered if he had ended the call entirely. I weighed my options. I could stay home with my parents and fight the urge to open up my laptop. Given the cold temperatures, I wasn't sure what I would really do to occupy my time. Or, I could give in to Miles' plan. We could all go stay at Opal Peak for the night and easily be back tomorrow by dinnertime.

We had all made a promise, to new memories and to make time for our friendship again.

"Okay, I'm in," I told both of them after we all sat in elongated silence.

"Wait, really?" Miles paused for a beat, letting out a nervous laugh. "You're always the voice of reason. You don't think this is a stupid idea?"

"No. I actually think it might be a good idea."

There was a pregnant pause from Miles. "Julian, are you still there?"

Julian's voice was quiet yet hoarse when he finally spoke. "I'll go."

"You guys are the best," Miles said with the same amount of excitement and high energy he had when we were younger. I couldn't help but feel a twinge of guilt for not seeking either of them out to meet up more often than the occasional visit when we were all back in Delmont Ridge. "You have two hours to get ready and then I'll be there to pick each of you up."

"You're not driving," Julian interjected. "I do not trust your ability to keep us alive on any of these mountain roads."

I couldn't help but smile, ducking my head as I turned away from my mother. She was watching me with such curiosity. "Two hours. I can do that. You two figure out who is driving."

I abruptly ended the call, feeling a giddiness spreading through me. It felt foreign.

My mother neatly folded her hands on her lap as I set her book back down onto the table and grabbed my mug of cold coffee.

"Leave it, I will get it," she said simply with a smile as she tucked her feet up underneath her. "Go get your things ready."

I stared at her for a moment. "I'm here to spend time with you guys for the holiday. You're really okay with me being gone for practically two days."

She nodded. "Life is too short, Raegan. Time is fleeting. Go have fun."

"I'll be home for Christmas," I assured her before disappearing from the room to pack my bag for the night.

I shouldn't be surprised with Miles throwing this on us out of nowhere. I couldn't help but smile. This was the Miles I always remembered.

And the one I was always drawn to.

CHAPTER FOUR

The guys were true to their word and it was almost exactly two hours later that they were standing outside of my parents' front door. My mother was in the kitchen and my father had since left for work when I walked to the door and pulled it open. Miles and Julian were both standing there with their hands tucked into the pockets of their winter coats.

Julian had a black beanie pulled down over his wavy onyx hair. Miles' cheeks were tinted red from the cold air, but he lacked a hat. I looked back and forth between them.

"Are you ready to go?" Miles asked.

"Where is your coat?" Julian spoke at the same time.

I tilted my head to the side as I looked at Julian for a moment. "It's inside. I just need to grab it and then I'll be ready to go."

"Where are your things?" he questioned me as I turned around and stepped back into the house. Julian was the first to move, walking behind me with Miles trailing along after him.

My mother stepped into the foyer, just as I was digging my old thick puffy coat from the closet. "Hi, Julian and Miles. It's so good to see the both of you."

"Hi Mrs. Thompson," they both said simultaneously.

I slid my arms into my coat and grabbed a pair of gloves and a hat before making my way to the base of the steps. Grabbing my bag, I lifted it into the air, but instead of slinging the strap over my shoulder, I pushed it against Julian's chest.

He raised a dark eyebrow at me.

"You asked where my things are. Here they are."

Miles snorted out a laugh, my mother half rolled her eyes and half laughed, and Julian just stared at me as he took the bag in his hands.

"We'll have her back tomorrow evening," Miles told my mother as I quickly stepped into the garage to grab my ski bag. It had my ski jacket, pants, goggles, helmet, gaiter, and gloves inside. I had a set of skis resting along the wall of the garage and Miles walked inside after me and grabbed them. Julian had disappeared out to his car and my mother was opening the garage door for us.

Miles carried the rest of my stuff out to the car and I turned to face my mother. "Are you sure this is okay?"

"Absolutely," she said with a warm smile as she

pulled me in for a hug. "Just have fun and be safe, okay? I love you."

"I love you too," I told her as she took a step back. I couldn't help but feel a bit guilty for leaving her to go away for the night when I was supposed to be here spending time with my family, but at the same time, I didn't miss the joy that was written across her face.

This was what my mother wanted for me. She wanted me to enjoy life and to actually live it.

I looked at Julian's car as I was making my way down the driveway and toward the street. Julian was standing by his door, leaning against the hood while Miles was holding the back door open for me. They were watching me and I shivered under both of their gazes. There was a touch of a fire burning in Miles' eyes as I slid into the car and he shut the door.

The look in Julian's was indistinguishable, but it still sent a spark of electricity down my spine. I pulled my seat belt on as they both got into their seats in the front. Julian was silent, only adjusting the rear view mirror until it was focused on me instead of the road. I studied his expression through the mirror, but he wasn't looking at me. His eyes were on the road as he pulled the car away from the curb.

Miles found the resort in his GPS and showed his phone to Julian while telling him the first few sets of directions. Julian reached into the center console and pulled out one of those little phone holders that slide into car vents. After putting it in place, he grabbed his own phone and pulled the directions up before putting it into the phone holder.

"Was there something wrong with my phone?" Miles asked him with a bit of annoyance in his tone.

Julian gave him a sideways glance. "No. Connect yours to the car and put on some music instead."

I looked back and forth between them. There was such a stark contrast in their attitudes, but that was how things always were between Miles and Julian. The most unlikely friends, yet it worked.

"I'm glad to see that you guys haven't changed at all."

Miles turned around in his seat to look at me. "What do you mean?"

"You two always argued like an old married couple and you still do," I told him with a smile as I shook my head. "You guys are like a couple out of a grumpy-sunshine romance novel. You're the sunshine one, while Julian is the grumpy one. He's always moody and broody, but you just take him as he is."

Julian's gaze met mine through the rearview mirror. He lifted an eyebrow. "We are not like a couple from a romance novel."

"You really are, though." I laughed and winked at him before looking back at Miles who genuinely looked curious. "It's kind of cute and weirdly refreshing."

"So, you think our bromance is cute?"

Julian shot a glare at Miles. "We do not have a bromance."

Miles rolled his eyes at Julian and ignored his response while he turned his attention back to me. "You didn't answer my question."

I looked again between them. Miles was staring at me expectantly, waiting for a response. Julian kept his eyes on the road, as if he was done with the two of us. I couldn't help but smile to myself. It was easy to get under his skin and it was kind of fun getting a bit of a rise out of him. If there were two people who had the ability to do that to Julian, it was Miles and I.

He used to get so irritated with us when we were younger, but there was always a hint of amusement dancing within his gaze as he watched the two of us. It was almost as if he were afraid to allow himself to be playful. Julian was the eldest child in his family, so he really played into the serious protector role. He needed to loosen up a bit and just relax.

It wasn't like he was afraid something was going to happen. The Julian Foster I knew was always fearless. He just bordered more on the line of quiet and serious. I could never quite figure out why, except for the fact that he had this need to make sure everyone was good. And that meant he didn't get to have fun like the rest of us.

"Yes, Miles. What the two of you have is adorable."

Julian snorted and Miles smiled brightly before turning to face his friend. "I told you we have a bromance."

Julian looked at him from the corner of his eye. "I never agreed to any of this."

"I don't think you ever had much of a choice," I told him as I stared into the mirror and shrugged.

"Nope," Miles agreed as he unlocked his phone and connected it to the car. He began to scroll through his Spotify playlists.

Julian's eyes lifted to mine through the rearview mirror. He studied me for a moment as mischief danced within the flames of his dark eyes. "I suppose I never really did."

My breath caught in my throat and a shiver slid down my spine with the way he stared at me. His gaze didn't waver and he didn't pull away at first. Music began to play through the speakers as Miles settled on a song as Julian's eyes lingered for a moment longer.

He looked back to the road while Miles turned the music up louder and got comfortable in his seat. I turned my head to look out the window as Julian pulled the car onto the highway that led up the mountain. We were only about ten minutes into our drive and the tension was already so thick in the small space. Thankfully, we were driving to a higher altitude where it would maybe thin out a bit.

Everyone just had pent-up energy from it being the winter months. As soon as we hit the slopes, it was bound to dissipate. And then perhaps I could relax around them instead of feeling like I was back in high school with damn butterflies fluttering around in my stomach. The attraction was always there, but we were all friends. There were different things I liked about them.

I knew in my heart and soul that I could never choose between Miles and Julian, and I would never put either of them in a position where any of us had to choose. I just buried my attraction and my feelings deep inside and pushed away the memories of any time I was close with either of them like they didn't exist.

Things were different now. We were all older, more mature, and knew what we wanted in life. And now the three of us were about to spend the night together on the mountain.

Perhaps this was a terrible idea…

But it was a little too late to turn around now.

CHAPTER FIVE

Miles checked in at the reception desk and got the key cards before meeting Julian and I by the elevators. We all stepped inside and it was borderline suffocating with the tension. Julian remained silent, staring ahead, while Miles whistled to himself like he didn't have a damn care in the world. I slid down the zipper of my coat and the sound practically echoed in the silence. Heat crept across my cheeks and I simply ducked my head and stared down at the floor.

The elevator doors slid open when we reached the eighth floor. Miles stepped out first and led the way down the hallway to our room. Julian and I stood behind him when he reached our room and waited for the beep as he held his key card to the small pad on the door. It sounded and Miles pushed it open, motioning for us to go ahead.

"Okay, so I got us a room with two queens and a pull-out couch. That way no one has to feel weird about the sleeping arrangement—" Miles paused as he saw Julian and I staring at the small room. "What the hell?"

I turned to look at him. "You were saying?"

"This is not the room I booked," he said with a frustrated sigh before looking between the two of us. Julian simply ignored him as he took my bag from me and sat them down by the closet door. "There's supposed to be three different spots to sleep... not one."

I looked away from him and back to the king-sized bed that occupied most of the space in the room. "Yeah... it looks like they maybe didn't hear you correctly."

Miles already had his phone out and was scrolling through his email for the reservation. He opened it up and showed it to me. "Look. Two queens and a pull-out couch." He glanced at Julian who had since made his way over to the floor-to-ceiling windows that lined one wall, overlooking the snow-covered mountains.

"Maybe try calling down to the front desk and see if they can move us to the room you had reserved?"

Miles nodded. "Good idea."

I moved over to one of the armchairs in the room and took a seat while Miles sat down on the bed. I glanced back at Julian. He turned around to face us, leaning back against the window with his arms crossed over his chest and one foot lazily crossed over the other. Heat spread through the pit of my stomach at the image of him and I quickly diverted my gaze back to Miles.

Miles dialed the front desk and put it on speaker-phone for Julian and I to hear. The woman who checked us into the resort answered after the third ring.

"How may I help you?"

Miles cleared his throat. "Hi, my name is Miles Walker. I had a reservation for the night for a room with two queen-sized beds and a pull-out couch. We're currently in room 816, which is not the room I reserved. This room only has one king-sized bed."

The woman was silent for a beat. "My apologies, Mr. Walker. Let me look into that right now. And I'm so sorry for the mishap, I'll see what we can do to correct this."

Julian grumbled something under his breath and Miles simply cut his eyes at him before rolling them. The woman had put him on hold and there was light Christmas music playing through the speaker. Miles began to hum and bob his head along to the tune.

Suddenly the music stopped and the woman's voice came back through the phone. "Mr. Walker. I'm not sure how things got mixed up in our system and, unfortunately, there is nothing we can do about it. With it being the holiday season, we're extremely busy and don't have a single room open for tonight."

Miles looked at me, his eyes wide. "So, the three of us are supposed to sleep in this room that doesn't even have a damn couch?"

"This should be interesting," Julian said, his voice low and barely audible from behind me. The sound slid across my eardrums and I fought to ignore the butterflies that fluttered in my stomach.

"I truly do apologize, Mr. Walker. Let me speak with my manager and see if there's any way we can comp the room for you tonight or add on a free night for tomorrow."

They ended the call and Miles looked between Julian and I. "Well, fuck... this wasn't how I planned our stay to be here."

"It's fine, Miles," I told him as I stood up from where I was sitting. "We're wasting time when we could be out there." I pointed out to the mountains. "We can just figure it out later, okay?"

"Okay, okay, you're right."

Julian was already moving around the room, getting his things. He stopped and looked between us before his gaze settled on me. "You said we are wasting time, so let's go."

His voice was quiet and commanding. Miles huffed as he rose to his feet and got ready to go. My feet refused to move. I was momentarily frozen beneath Julian's dark gaze. He watched me with an indistinguishable look in his eye. Swallowing roughly, I forced myself to get ready and it wasn't long before the three of us were heading back out into the hallway.

I fell into step beside Miles, but I could feel Julian's

eyes on me the entire time. As we walked, while we were in the elevator, and as we headed down to the ski shop. When we hit the slopes, Julian seemed less than interested in the actual act of skiing. He had always made it look easy and was effortless with the way he moved.

But those damn midnight eyes...

Every time I looked at him, they were focused on nothing other than me.

———

"Well, I don't know about either of you, but I'm ready to get some food and drinks," Miles said to Julian and me as the three of us all carried our skis back to the area in the shop where guests were able to store them.

The sun had already begun to set and the clouds in the sky were dark as snow flurries began to fall. They were thick and big, but they fell with ease. It wasn't uncommon for Colorado, especially in the mountains. The sky looked angry, like there was an impending storm. I hadn't even thought to check the weather until that moment.

Miles took my skis and set them down with his before coming back over to me. He looked up at the sky to where the snowflakes were falling a bit faster. "Shit. Were we supposed to get a lot of snow?"

I shrugged. "I didn't check the weather at all. I'm guessing you didn't either?"

"We're in Opal Peak," Julian said with simplicity as he walked past us. "Would you expect it not to snow?"

Miles rolled his eyes at the back of Julian's head as he held his arm out for me. I linked mine through his and we followed the moody, broody friend of ours, back into the building. "Hopefully it isn't much snow. I did promise your mother that I would have you back by dinner tomorrow."

There was nothing strange about the way we were walking together. If anything, it felt right, like my arm was exactly where it was supposed to be. Miles smelled like snow and cedarwood and I reveled in his warmth with how close he was to me. Damn them both for having such an effect on me. I had no choice but to shove it away.

"I think we should be okay. You know how unpredictable the weather is here."

"True," Miles agreed as we made our way back up to the room to change. "And it's not like we didn't grow up driving in snow."

"Exactly." I smiled at him as he stepped away. "We'll be fine."

Miles winked at me and the butterflies fluttered. "We'll be more than fine."

We all quickly changed out of the clothes we wore to ski all day, each taking turns in the bathroom. I freshened up the light makeup I had on my eyes and slipped into an oversized sage green sweater, a pair of black leggings, and boots. Both of the guys were waiting by the door for me and I stopped and smiled at the sight of them.

They were both relatively even in height, standing about a foot above me. Julian watched me with his dark eyes while Miles watched me with his light ones. My yin and yang. A few strands of Julian's inky hair hung across his forehead and Miles' was a mess of curls on top of his head. I swallowed roughly, telling my heart to stop hammering away in my chest as I walked up to them.

"Shall we?"

Miles stepped to the side and waved me through them. "After you, my lady."

As I walked between them, my shoulders brushed theirs. I couldn't help myself from inhaling deeply as both of their scents penetrated my senses. Miles like cedarwood and moss, and Julian like sandalwood. I couldn't let myself go there. I quickly recovered and moved out into the hall with them trailing behind me.

The three of us headed down to the bar and found a booth to sit in. Miles ordered a pitcher of beer and got three mugs that he filled to the brim for each of us. We all slowly sipped as we waited for the server to order some food. I needed to eat something, but I was ready to swallow enough alcohol to make me fall into a dead sleep.

Tonight was going to be a long-ass night and the last thing I wanted to do was make a mistake with either one of them I might regret in the morning. I already knew that I was in fucking trouble with the three of us sharing a room with one damn bed.

I knew both of them well enough to know they would both offer to sleep on the floor and leave the bed for me.

And they knew I wouldn't let them sleep on the ground when there was room for all of us in the bed.

Fuck me.

CHAPTER SIX

I had lost count of how many beers I had to drink. The dinner I ate was definitely helping because I wasn't as drunk as I could have been. But I was well on my way to getting there, which was the plan when we walked into the bar. Miles had gotten up a few minutes ago to go to the bathroom, leaving Julian and I alone while he was taking his sweet time.

Julian's dark eyes were on me and I had my beer muscles on. His eyes were always on me and I did my best to ignore it, but that self-control had since flown out the window. My filter was officially gone and I wasn't holding back any longer.

"Why are you staring at me?" I paused for a beat. "As a matter of fact, why are you always staring at me like that?"

Julian casually sipped his beer and tilted his head to the side. "In what way are you referring to?"

Him and his fucking responses. I let out an exasperated sigh. "I don't know how to even explain it. You just have this look, and you're doing it right now."

He chuckled softly. "Perhaps I enjoy looking at beautiful things, Raegan."

My breath caught in my throat and my eyes widened as I stared back at him. He did not just say that. That had to have been a figment of my imagination. Or perhaps he was feeling the alcohol settling into his veins like I was.

"You don't mean that."

Julian's face remained expressionless but I didn't miss the wave of confusion that passed through his eyes. "Why would you say that?"

Closing my eyes, I ran my hand down my face in a dramatic fashion. "Do I really need to bring this up right now?"

If I knew what was good for me, I would have shut my damn mouth right then and there. When I said I wanted to get drunk, I simply just wanted to be able to sleep in peace tonight. I didn't mean I wanted to do it to spill my hidden feelings onto the table.

"I'm not quite sure what you're talking about. Of course I meant what I said, Raegan." He folded his arms on the table and leaned on them as his gaze penetrated mine. "I won't apologize for staring at you when I simply can't help myself. You're beautiful. Always have been."

I stared at him, half in disbelief, half just because I

was progressively feeling more drunk as time passed. "You let me kiss you. You kissed me back. And then you pushed me away because you had a girlfriend."

Regret flashed in his eyes. "I regret that more than you'll ever understand."

His words felt like a blow to my chest. I was fairly certain that I winced, or maybe I just imagined myself making the face. Julian's eyebrows pulled together, like he wasn't understanding the reasoning behind my reaction. I let out another sigh and leaned back against my seat in an effort to cover up the pain that was still piercing my heart.

"Do you think maybe you should go check on Miles?"

Julian's face was unreadable and he glanced over to the bar. "He's right over there."

Turning sideways in my seat, I looked over to where Julian was staring. Miles was leaning against the bar, talking to some other girl with bright blonde hair. She was drop-dead gorgeous and Miles was sporting that charming grin he wore when he was working his magic on someone. A flame of jealousy sparked inside me.

I couldn't tear my eyes away from them. The girl put her hand on Miles' forearm and her head tipped back as she let out a string of laughter. My eyebrows were scrunched in a scowl. He was supposed to be here with us. I knew my jealousy was a little unwarranted and a tad out of pocket, but I couldn't help it. This was supposed to be our night here. Our night together, making new memories and rekindling our friendship.

There was a part of me that knew the alcohol in my system had nothing to do with these feelings. It had to do with the feelings I had for Miles that I kept buried deep inside. The alcohol was just drawing them out and making sure everyone else knew my secrets.

My nostrils flared and I pushed up from my seat at the booth. My body swayed slightly and the room shifted. Shit. I sat back down and chugged some of the water that had magically appeared on the table at some point during the night.

"Are you okay?" Julian questioned me, his voice soft and tender.

I narrowed my eyes at him. "He's supposed to be with us, not with whoever the hell she is."

Julian chuckled again as mischief danced in his irises. "Miles is a big boy. He's free to do whatever he pleases."

"Um, no, he isn't. Remember, this was all his idea. He doesn't get to just ditch us now."

Julian studied me. "You're jealous."

"No, I'm not," I argued before slugging some more water. I needed to sober up. "Maybe I am."

"Interesting," Julian mused as he cocked his head to the side. There was a deep curiosity in his eyes and I wanted to reach out and wipe it away. He didn't get to assess me on this. So what if I was attracted to both of my friends?

"Are you judging me?"

"Quite the contrary," he retorted. "I had my suspicions…"

I scowled at him. "What suspicions?"

A wicked grin pulled on his lips. "That you had a thing for both of us."

My eyes widened. There's no way he could have known. His suspicions? Had I really been that obvious? Part of me cared, the other didn't in the moment. I knew in the morning I would be regretting this conversation immensely. I'd probably want to go bury myself in the snow, but it would be okay. We'd gotten over awkward moments in the past, there was no reason why we couldn't do that now.

"Go get your boy," Julian said with a wink. "I think it's been a long day and we could all use some sleep."

My lips parted and I abruptly shut them as I remembered the predicament we were in with our sleeping situation. I looked back over at Miles and the girl. Her hand was still on his arm and they were standing relatively close. Gone were the thoughts of the one-bed ordeal. I rose to my feet, feeling a little less wobbly, and let them carry me straight in the direction of the bar.

"There you are," I said sweetly as I stepped up to Miles and the blonde. Miles turned to look at me, his face lighting up as he drank me in with his gaze.

"Hey you," he replied, his voice as smooth as honey. He threw his arm around the tops of my shoulders and pulled me against him, pressing his lips to the top of my head. "Did you miss me?"

The butterflies fluttered in my stomach. "I did. Are you ready to head upstairs?"

"Absolutely," he said with a smile before looking back at the girl. "Enjoy the rest of your trip."

She looked between the two of us, her eyes slicing to mine with an icy glare. "Yeah, you too."

I couldn't help the boost of confidence I felt, along with the satisfaction that mixed with it. The look on that girl's face was absolutely priceless. I was most definitely on her shit list for tearing him away from her, but he didn't even hesitate when I stepped over to him.

His arm dropped down to wrap around my waist and we half stumbled out of the bar together. I didn't see Julian anywhere, so I figured he had headed up to the room already. Miles and I walked over to the elevator and he pressed the up button.

He turned me in his arms, both of his hands resting on my hips. "Thank you for saving me. I couldn't figure out a nice way to get away from her."

I smiled up at him. "It was my pleasure."

His light eyes twinkled. "If I'm being honest, there wasn't a part of that whole thing I didn't like. Almost like you came over to claim your territory."

"What if I did?"

Miles stepped closer, lifting one hand to brush a stray hair away from my face. "Raegan... fuck. We always said we wouldn't do anything to ruin our friendship."

I wasn't sure what had come over me. Perhaps I needed an exorcism because something was possessing me. I needed him closer. He was overwhelming and consuming. I lifted my arms to link them around the back of his neck.

"What if we're doing the opposite of ruining it?"

His jaw tightened and his throat bobbed as he swallowed roughly. His eyes bounced back and forth between mine once.

"Fuck it," he growled before crushing his lips against mine.

CHAPTER SEVEN

Miles' mouth was against mine without a single ounce of hesitation or restraint. His lips were soft and warm, moving with a tenderness. My hands gripped the front of his shirt, needing to feel him closer as his tongue slid along the seam of my lips. I slowly parted them, letting him in, and there was a shift between us in the way he kissed me.

His tongue slid against mine and I moaned into his mouth, unable to help myself. His fingertips dug into my skin as his grip tightened on my waist. He was everywhere, consuming me, kissing me with such an intensity I could feel it crackling through my bones like electricity.

His hands were in my dark brown hair, holding the base of my head as he tipped it back farther to grant him more access. His tongue moved with mine with perfect precision. The elevator behind us dinged and all it took was that sound to bring us crashing back to reality. We abruptly broke apart as Miles pulled back. We were both left breathless and he stared down at me with a fire burning in his eyes.

"Raegan..." His voice was hoarse and thick with lust as he stared down at me. "Fuck."

I stared back up at him, still feeling the rush of his lips against mine. Adrenaline coursed through my veins, mixing with the alcohol that still had me feeling like I was in a daze. I couldn't separate the two and my body was warm with need. I clenched my thighs together.

"Are you both coming?"

Julian.

His voice broke through the silence and Miles didn't move away from me, still cupping the sides of my face as he glanced over his shoulder at Julian. I shifted to the side, my eyes meeting Julian's from where he was standing in the elevator. He was leaning against the wall with his hands tucked in his front pockets, watching the two of us with lucid curiosity.

Miles turned back to me with a smirk and stepped away, his hands falling from my face. He grabbed my wrist and pulled me into the elevator with them. I was sandwiched between Miles and Julian. No one moved, no one spoke a single word. We just stood there as the doors slid shut.

The tension was palpable and the air was suffocating.

Julian was the first to move. He stepped forward, but he didn't press the button for our floor. Instead, he turned around to face Miles and me. His eyes met mine first and darkness danced with the flames in his irises. He glanced at Miles and I looked at him from the corner of my eye. A smirk lifted his lips and he released my wrist as he nodded.

Julian's eyes were back on mine as he stalked toward me, closing the small amount of distance between us in the elevator. My breath caught in my throat. Time was momentarily suspended. My mind couldn't comprehend what the hell was going on.

He just saw Miles and I kiss and now he was stalking toward me like I was his prey.

His toes reached mine and he lifted his hands, planting them on either side of my head on the elevator wall as he caged me in. I couldn't breathe and I wasn't sure I even wanted to. Those flames in his eyes threatened to consume me. I watched, frozen in place, as his tongue darted out to wet his lips.

Lifting one hand from the wall, he placed his two fingers just beneath my jaw. "Your heart's pounding, Raegan." His voice was low and seductive. My thighs clenched again as the warmth in my body spread. "Is it from Miles," he murmured as he trailed his fingers up to press them to my lips. He slowly dragged them down my chin and along the column of my throat. "Or is it from me?"

My lips parted and a ragged breath finally escaped me.

"Perhaps it's from both of us," Miles mused from where he was standing beside me.

Julian lightly wrapped his hand around the nape of my neck. "Tell me, sweetheart. Is your heart about to break through your rib cage from both of us?"

Holy fuck.

His voice was demanding, yet there was a tenderness in his tone. His touch was burning my flesh. Pulling my bottom lip between my teeth, I bit down and nodded. There was no denying it, not with the way my body was responding. And my brain lacked any sense of control as I was caught under his spell.

"You're waiting for me to kiss you, aren't you?"

I stared up at him as he towered over me. I wasn't sure I wanted him to kiss me, because I was afraid I was possibly going to combust. But I did. It was practically a sin with how badly I wanted to feel his lips against mine.

"I'm just wondering what exactly you're waiting for," I countered.

A soft chuckle escaped him. He pressed his pelvis against me, pinning me against the wall of the elevator. We still hadn't moved. I forgot we were even supposed to be going to our room. I glanced past him, noticing that Miles had moved over to where the panel of buttons were beside the door. A devious smirk played on his lips as he casually watched the two of us.

"I'm waiting for you to make a move, sweetheart," he murmured as his face dipped closer to mine. His breath was but a whisper away from my lips. "You're in control here, not me. I just saw you and Miles kiss and as badly as I want a taste for myself, I don't know if you only want him or if you want me too."

He wanted my honesty and that was the one thing the three of us had always given one another. I wasn't sure what this would do to our friendship, but I wasn't quite sure I cared anymore. After having an attraction to my two best friends that only grew over the years, I was done playing it safe. I was here to live my life, not to keep letting it pass me by.

"I want you both."

"Fuck." Miles let out a sharp breath from where he was standing.

Julian's dark eyes glimmered under the lights in the elevator. The corners of his lips twitched. "That's my girl."

His lips brushed against mine, teasing me in the slowest possible way. My knees felt weak. My breath was caught in my throat, anticipation was coursing through my veins. Would he or wouldn't he kiss me? It was absolutely maddening and slowly killing me.

My eyelids fluttered shut as he softly pressed his lips to the corner of my mouth. He brushed his nose against mine before kissing the other corner. I groaned and my shoulders sagged as a chuckle rumbled in his chest. "So impatient."

I abruptly grabbed the side of his face and pulled it to mine. He didn't fight me, he didn't hesitate, and his mouth crashed into mine. His hips shifted, grinding his erection against my stomach as he kept me pressed against the wall. His hand moved to the front of my neck. Using his thumb, he tilted my chin up while gripping my throat with his fingers.

My lips parted without warning and Julian's tongue slid into my mouth, tasting and teasing me. I wasn't sure I was breathing anymore. It didn't matter anyway. He drew the oxygen from my lungs, kissing me until I was weak on my feet. My body threatened to melt into a puddle.

I was dizzy from the lack of oxygen, the alcohol, his lips, and Miles' eyes. It was almost too much yet not enough. Such a contradiction, yet I wanted more. I wanted it all… from both of them.

Julian's lips felt like they were bruising my own, like when he finally pulled away his mark would be stained on my mouth for an eternity. I didn't care. It was brutal yet gentle. Rough yet soft. He was obliterating my thoughts, muddling my mind. There was nothing rushed with the way he kissed me. It was like he had all the time in the world and wasn't going to rush it.

And then his lips were gone.

In an instant, he pulled back and the elevator dinged. I hadn't even realized we were moving. At some point, Miles must have decided to press the floor number and we had reached it.

Julian's hand was still on my throat and his gaze crashed into mine.

"You misunderstood me earlier."

My eyebrows scrunched together. "What do you mean?"

"The other time we kissed, when I said I regret that more than you'll ever understand…"

My stomach sank at his words as the memory seeped back into my clouded thoughts. Julian didn't move away, still keeping me pinned against the wall, caging me in.

"I didn't regret kissing you, Raegan. I regretted that I stopped. I regretted letting you walk away instead of instantly calling Erin to end things with her."

My eyes widened and I stared back at him, completely speechless. Julian released me and took a step back. My knees half buckled and I swayed on my feet. "What?"

"Shh," Julian said as he stepped closer and slid his arm around my waist, pulling me away from the wall. "Let's get you to bed. And if you remember this conversation in the morning, I'll tell you whatever you want to know."

My eyes flashed to Miles' as he stood by the door, holding it open for us. "I have questions for you too."

Miles laughed softly. "I didn't do anything. I wasn't the one who kissed you when I had a girlfriend."

"Yeah, but…" My voice trailed off as they led me down the hallway to our room. "I'm really confused by all of this. How is this not weird?"

"Because it's us," Julian murmured against my ear as he helped me into the room. He led me over to the bed and Miles pulled back the comforter as Julian set me down on the mattress. Miles dropped to his knees and pulled off my shoes before I scooted up to the pillows. As I laid down, Julian dragged the blankets up to my chin. "Sleep, sweetheart. We'll talk tomorrow."

"Neither of you ever made a real move before because we weren't supposed to mess up our friend-ship… but now both of you at the same time?"

Miles laughed again. "This is a conversation for tomorrow, Rae. Maybe Julian and I finally came to our senses and decided we'd rather share than fight over who gets you all to themselves."

I stared at them. "This is fucking weird." I paused as Miles grabbed a spare pillow and dropped it onto the floor. Julian was already walking over to a closet and digging through it. "What are you guys doing?"

"Getting stuff to make our beds on the floor."

My mouth opened wide as I yawned. "Don't be foolish. There's room in the bed for all three of us." I grabbed two pillows and put one on either side of me. "Look, I'm even safe from both of you this way."

"A pillow wouldn't fucking stop me, sweetheart," Julian mumbled as he shut the closet door.

Miles stared at me for a second. "Are you sure?"

"Yes. Just shut up and lay down. I want to sleep."

Julian chuckled and they climbed into the bed, both men laying on either side of me. For a moment, my mind raced with how close they were, sending my senses into overdrive, but it didn't take long for the alcohol to pull me into the depths of sleep.

And I was lost in the darkness with both of them floating through my dreams.

CHAPTER EIGHT

The bed was warm. *Too warm.* I went to shift on the mattress, to roll over onto my side, and my leg wouldn't move. It was stuck... between someone else's legs. My eyelids flew open and I blinked rapidly against the harsh light shining in through the window. My head throbbed in protest and I ignored the pounding feeling as I turned my head to the side. It was the owner of the legs that had mine trapped between his.

Miles.

He snored lightly and didn't move as I used all my strength to free my leg from his. Only when I went to move did I realize the reasoning behind why I was so damn warm. An arm shifted over my waist and I quickly turned my head to the other side, only to be face to face with Julian.

Miles was facing the other direction with his back

pressed against my side and Julian was laying facing me with his arm now around my waist. My mind was cloudy as hell and I quickly sifted through my memories of the night before.

I took a sharp breath, inhaling both of their scents. The night came crashing back to me and I remembered it all. The three of us going to the bar, Julian and I talking about what happened when I went to see him in Italy. Miles and the other girl at the bar. Me being pretty tipsy and getting jealous. The two of us kissing by the elevator. And Julian pinning me against the wall in the elevator as he kissed me senseless after Miles.

This had to have been a dream. They both admitted they wanted me last night, that they wanted to share me—in no reality would this ever actually be happening to me.

I looked past Julian, my eyes widening as I realized why it was so bright outside. The sun was shining, but it was illuminating the snow that covered everything outside. Large, fluffy snowflakes were still falling from the sky in rapid succession.

Grabbing Julian's shoulder, I shook him. His body was heavy and barely moved, but slowly, he peeled open his eyelids and stared at me through the small slits. "What?"

"It's snowing outside."

"Okay... it's winter, Raegan. That's usually what happens."

Miles stirred beside me and I could feel his body as

he rolled to face the two of us. "What are you guys going on about?"

"Raegan is the new weather girl," Julian offered before shutting his eyes again to block out the harsh light.

"You guys are both assholes," I muttered as I shoved them away from me and pulled the comforter off the bed as I climbed off.

"What the hell?" Miles groaned and attempted to scoot closer to Julian who pushed him away. "I'm cold."

"I don't care," Julian said and slowly sat up to look at me. "We don't have to check out for another hour. Please come back to bed or return the comforter so we can go back to sleep for a little while."

I wandered over to the window, dread pooling in the pit of my stomach as I got a better look outside. Everything was literally covered in white. The small snowstorm from last night turned out to not be so small. We thought it would stop, but it didn't. It must have continued throughout the night and it was still snowing now.

"I don't think we're going to be checking out today."

I turned back to face them as Miles slowly sat up. "What do you mean?"

"Come see for yourself," I told them and pointed outside before walking in the opposite direction into the bathroom. I couldn't hear their voices as I brushed my teeth, but I knew they were coming to the same realization I had come to. We weren't going to be able to get home for Christmas Eve tonight.

As I began to walk back out of the bathroom, I found them dressed in fresh clothes and Julian was heading in my direction. He brushed past me as he walked into the bathroom, but remained silent as he began to brush his teeth. Miles was right behind him and he paused as he reached me.

"Get dressed. We're going outside to see how bad it really is."

A sigh escaped me as I walked over to my bag and grabbed some clothes. I made sure to change quickly, before they reappeared from the bathroom. I didn't bring much with me, but I made sure to pack warm clothing. I was dressed and ready to go outside by the time they were done brushing their teeth and whatever else they were doing in there.

The three of us were silent as we left our room and caught the elevator to the first floor. The tension was thick and heavy in the air around us. The big elephant in the room was whiter than the damn snow outside. I wanted to bring it up, but I wasn't quite sure how. I wasn't sure if I was supposed to feel awkward or okay with it. Too many questions were flooding my mind. I decided it was better to choose silence and wait for one of them to address it first.

Although, I wasn't quite sure either of them were going to bring it up.

The air was cold as we stepped out into the parking

lot. My boots sunk in the snow and I pulled my hood up to block the flakes that were rapidly falling. Julian was leading the way with Miles close behind him and I was the last one walking over to the car. There was no way in hell we were going anywhere.

They must have plowed the parking lot at some point, but it was hard to tell anymore. The only thing that gave it away were the piles pushed off to the side, but the ground had since been re-covered in snow. It was at least six inches deep.

Julian stopped beside his car and brushed some of the snow away with his arm before pulling the door open. I stopped beside Miles, watching as he grabbed the ice scraper from inside and began to brush the snow away from the windows.

I looked over at Miles. "We're not getting out of here."

"Yeah… I think we might have to stay another night."

Julian glanced at us over his shoulder. "We've driven in worse conditions than this. We'll be fine."

Miles rolled his eyes and linked his arm through mine as he led me out of the way while Julian got inside his car. We waited while he started the engine and let it warm up for a minute or two. He put it in reverse and pressed on the gas, only to have his car stay in place. If anything, it shifted a few inches while the wheels spun.

Miles chuckled and I shook my head. "He's so damn

stubborn sometimes. He knew damn well this wouldn't work but needed to know for sure it wouldn't."

"Want to go see about getting that room for another night?" I asked him while Julian climbed out of the car.

"Absolutely," Miles said with a smile and a wink. "I'll meet you both back inside."

Miles left me standing there as I watched an irritated Julian slam the door of his car. He slowly turned to face me, his expression unreadable, but there was a scowl on his lips.

"We were supposed to get you home today. Your mother was expecting you."

I stared at him for a moment with my eyebrows pulling together. "It's fine, Julian. I'll call her and explain. I'm sure no one wants any of us trying to drive in this weather just to get home for Christmas Eve."

Julian fell silent. The scowl disappeared from his lips and his footsteps were deliberately slow as he stepped closer to me. He stopped just as he reached me, his head tilting down to meet my gaze.

"Do you remember last night?"

His question struck me in the chest. Heat crept up my neck and spread across my face as the memories flooded my mind again. I nodded. "I do. And I believe you said that if I remembered, you would tell me anything I wanted to know."

His eyes were focused on mine. "I did."

I was terrified to walk through the door we left hanging wide open last night. "You said you regretted letting me walk away and not breaking up with her then. Why?"

"Isn't it obvious?" He paused for a moment, tilting his head to the side as the corners of his mouth twitched. "Hasn't it always been obvious? I only ever had eyes for you, Raegan. But I knew Miles had feelings for you too. It was too messy, too risky. I was a coward. I didn't want to ruin our friendship and I didn't want to lose you at the same time."

The oxygen left my lungs in a rush. My eyes widened and I was rendered speechless. No, it wasn't obvious... not to me, at least. They were both always protective of me, but I always thought it was coming from a platonic stance.

"I just don't understand what changes things now," I said quietly, not fully trusting my voice. "With both of you."

Julian let out a sigh and ran a hand through his snow-dusted inky hair. "I feel like we've always been dancing around one another. I'm tired of wasting time because I'm afraid of what may or may not happen. Maybe it all blows up in our faces—who knows. But I do know one thing... we won't know if we don't explore the possibilities."

I stared at him for a moment. "What about Miles?"

A smirk played on his lips. "I only speak for myself. You'll have to ask him your own questions." He slowly slid his hand into mine and turned me with him to face the building. "Let's go see if he was able to get the room for tonight. I don't particularly care to sleep in my car tonight."

"One last question," I said as I pulled him to a stop.

Julian turned back to face me. "Of course, sweetheart."

"Did you and Miles already talk about this?"

His dark irises shimmered. "We did."

"And you decided you'd rather share?"

A soft chuckle escaped him. "He's my best friend, Raegan, but he isn't going to get the girl I've been wanting since we were in high school. If he wants her too, then it's only fair that we share."

I couldn't believe we were having this conversation right now. Not that I was opposed to the idea. I was just a little... shocked, to say the least.

"Is it too early for a drink?"

His head tipped back as laughter spilled from his lips. "Come on, sweetheart." He pulled me back beside him and I fell into step with him as we walked back to the resort. "Let's get you a drink and the rest of your answers."

"I don't need any more answers. Just a drink."

He glanced at me and winked. "Your wish is my command."

CHAPTER NINE

When we reached the front desk, Miles was talking to the same woman from the day before. As we walked up to him, he began to turn around with a smile on his face. Julian and I stopped short and Miles met us toward the center of the lobby instead.

"It just so happens that we're in luck. We're able to have the room for another night and because of the mix-up from yesterday, it's free."

Julian nodded and I smiled back at Miles. "That's great news." I paused for a moment as I remembered what today was. "We should all probably call our parents to let them know we won't be back today."

"Yeah, that's probably a good idea," Miles agreed as he pulled his own phone out of his pocket. Julian had turned his back to us and was walking across the lobby with his phone pressed to his ear.

I watched Miles for a second as he began to talk to his mom. His light blue eyes met mine and he winked before he went over to sit on one of the armchairs by the fireplace along the wall in the lobby. My eyes followed after him and as he took his seat, his gaze collided with mine again but this time it didn't waver.

A shiver slid down my spine as the flames in his eyes matched the ones flickering beside him. Reaching into the pocket of my coat, I pulled out my phone and scrolled through my contacts. I found my mother's name and tapped on it as the call connected. I was the only one who remained in the center of the room as I waited for my mother to answer.

Her soft voice came through the speaker after the third ring. "Hello?"

"Hey, Mom."

"Raegan. Is everything okay? I heard there was a terrible snowstorm in Opal Peak." She paused for a moment. "You're okay, right?"

A soft laugh escaped me. "Yes, Mom. I'm fine, we're all fine, everything's okay." I let out an exasperated sigh as I wandered over to one of the couches in the lobby and took a seat. "It started snowing yesterday evening, but we thought it was something that would blow over. We just came in from Julian trying to move his car that's stuck in the parking lot."

"Well, shit," she muttered before letting out a string of laughter. "This isn't exactly ideal. This would happen the year we all decide to get together and do a big

Christmas. Thankfully, it's only Christmas Eve, though."

"I know, but I feel bad because I was supposed to come back home this afternoon so we could spend some time together."

My mother was silent for a beat. "None of that matters, Raegan. I would much rather you be stuck there and be safe rather than trying to travel when the roads aren't safe. We aren't going anywhere. We will wait for you all to get back before we do anything. I would hope the weather and the roads would clear up enough that you will be able to get back tomorrow sometime."

"That's what we were hoping. We were able to get our room for another night here, so we're just going to wait it out and see."

"As much as I want you here, I want you safe," my mother assured me with her voice warm and comforting. "We will make the most out of the time we have together and everything will be fine."

My mother was predictable in this way. She was always the calm and collected reassuring parent. Not much fazed her. She didn't get worked up about things and always believed there was some type of solution. Things didn't have to be hard in her mind. Whatever we had to do, we would always make it work.

"We will be home as soon as we can," I told her, catching Miles' eye again. He had since ended his phone call but was still seated by the fireplace. Julian was standing in front of him, but I couldn't hear what they were talking about from where I was sitting. "I will keep you posted."

"Just enjoy yourself, honey. I'll see you tomorrow."

"I love you, Mom," I said and she returned the sentiment before we ended the call.

Slowly rising to my feet, I walked across the sitting area over to where Miles and Julian were. They were still in deep conversation with their voices hushed. Miles' eyes tracked my movements as I made my way over and I watched his lips move, noticing my name fall from them as he mumbled something to Julian.

Julian turned around to face me as I reached them. His eyes were shining and the corners of his lips lifted into a small grin. "Everything good with your mom?"

I nodded, looking over at the massive Christmas tree beyond him. The lights twinkled, illuminating the ornaments hung among the branches. I directed my attention back to the two of them as they were waiting for my full response. "She was perfectly fine with it. She doesn't want us to risk anything by trying to get home tonight. I told her I would keep her posted on what happens and that we would be home tomorrow for Christmas."

"Mine basically said the same," Miles offered from where he was sitting.

"So did mine," Julian added.

I shifted my weight on my feet as I looked between them. "So, now what?"

A smirk played on Julian's lips. "How about we get you that drink you were saying you needed?"

"A drink already?" Miles laughed. "Isn't it a little early for that?"

"Not at all," I told him. "We haven't had breakfast yet and mimosas are perfect for any time of the day."

Miles rose to his feet and they both stepped to either side of me. "Let's go see where we can get you what you're looking for."

I half choked on the breath I was trying to inhale. I didn't have to go far to find what I was looking for...

———

We were all seated around a table, waiting for the breakfast we had ordered to be brought to us. I slowly sipped my mimosa while Julian did the same. Miles opted for a Bloody Mary, though the thought of vodka and tomato juice just never seemed appealing to me. The three of us had fallen into a conversation, talking about how it would be perfect to ski after the snow finished falling, but there was still the elephant in the room.

I had addressed it with Julian... kind of. But nothing had been said between Miles and I. It was a conversation that I wasn't sure how to approach and I couldn't help but feel a little strange with Julian sitting here as I considered bringing it up. The whole situation was fucking bizarre. I mean, I'm sure it was a lot of girls' dreams.

There was never a point in my life where I considered the possibility of having to choose one or the other when it came to Miles and Julian. It was something I never imagined happening with either of them, so the fact that they both wanted me and wanted to share me made it even more difficult to wrap my mind around. One of them never felt like an option…

I was still walking around in a bit of a shocked state. My mom's words rang in my head. She wanted me to live my life more instead of focusing on work. This wasn't how I pictured living my life would look, but it was time for me to stop playing everything safe. It was time to start taking risks.

And I was going to start with my two best friends.

"Miles." I said his name softly as there was a break in the conversation he and Julian had slipped into while I was lost in my own mind. "Julian and I already addressed the elephant in the room, but I have questions for you."

He tilted his head to the side, a mischievous grin playing on his lips. "What do you want to know, sweets? I'm sure Julian probably spoke enough for the both of us."

He was right. I didn't need any more confirmation from him. Between what happened last night and what Julian said this morning, it was confirmed. Miles wanted me just as badly as Julian did. But he was still my best friend and the last thing I wanted to do was ruin that if it wasn't something he was truly comfortable risking.

"Are you sure this is what you want?"

His eyebrows tugged together. "What do you mean?"

"Me," I said quietly, not fully trusting my voice. "Are you sure you want me when your best friend does too?"

"Oh, sweets." Miles smiled brightly, shaking his head as a chuckle rumbled in his chest. "I've wanted you since I *really* noticed you in high school. Since you transformed from our best friend to the girl every other guy was staring at with a bead of drool dripping from his mouth. It was a lot of fucking work chasing those assholes away."

"Wait... you guys are the reason why no one ever wanted to date me in high school?"

Julian laughed softly. "If we couldn't have you, they sure as fuck weren't going to."

"You guys are assholes." I snorted while rolling my eyes. I looked back to Miles, finding his eyes already on mine.

His blue eyes burned holes through mine. "To answer your question, I've never been more sure about anything else in my life."

I swallowed roughly as I glanced between them. "And you both want to share?"

"Sharing is caring." Miles smirked and winked at

me. "Yes, Raegan. Stop overthinking this shit. Just go with it and see where it takes all of us."

"Are you okay with this?" Julian asked me, his voice soft like velvet. "I know it's a little unconventional…"

My chest rose as I inhaled deeply, before exhaling slowly. My gaze shifted from Julian to Miles before returning to Julian.

"It's unconventional. It's uncharted territory, but I'm okay with this."

"Are you sure?" Miles questioned me this time.

A smile pulled on my lips as I repeated the same words back to him.

"I've never been more sure about anything else in my life."

CHAPTER TEN

Breakfast came to an interesting end before I told the guys I was going to go have a spa day. I needed some space from them. I needed to clear my head and since we were snowed in here, I decided I was going to pamper myself. Miles tried to come along, but Julian wouldn't let him. I silently thanked him and was extremely grateful to have the time to myself.

After all, the three of us were stuck here for another night, all sharing the same bedroom. With what we'd discussed lately, I had a feeling all this built-up tension was finally going to come to a head. There would be no avoiding it tonight after the three of us were back in the same room together.

I was still terrified to take the leap with them. What if things went badly? What if it didn't work out? What if it ruined our friendship?

I was laying on the table as the massage therapist was working the knots from my muscles. Letting my eyelids fall closed, I pushed the negative thoughts away from my mind. There was no sense in dwelling on the what-ifs. If Miles and Julian felt it was worth the risk, I had to trust them. They wouldn't set me up for failure and they weren't in the habit of self-sabotaging.

The rest of my day passed without any lingering thoughts. I tried my best to forget about Miles and Julian waiting for me to be done. I wasn't sure what they were doing with their day. They assured me they would find something to do when I mentioned wanting to go to the spa. They agreed I should go, that I deserved to be pampered.

After rinsing off, I changed back into my clothing and made my way to the front desk of the spa. There was a girl, probably in her early twenties, sitting at the reception area. She was there when I checked in this morning. She smiled brightly as I walked over to where I was to pay for the services I took advantage of here.

"How was your day here? I hope you're feeling refreshed and rejuvenated."

I smiled back at her, feeling the aftereffects of my massage still rippling through my body. I was thoroughly relaxed and feeling much looser than I was when I first walked in. In a way, it was almost an intoxicating feeling.

"I most definitely do. It was absolutely amazing."

She nodded. "That's what we love to hear. What's your name so I can get you checked out?"

I told her my name and she began to type it into the computer system as she looked for everything I had done. Her eyebrows pulled together and she tilted her head to the side before looking back at me. "It looks like everything has already been paid for."

I stared at her for a moment, my brow furrowing. "What do you mean?"

She grabbed the computer monitor and turned it so I could see. "Someone called earlier and spoke to my colleague Annie before she left and had it charged to the room."

I wasn't able to conceal the shock on my face. It took me a moment to recover and for the reality of it to set in. Either Miles or Julian had to have been the ones to call down to have it charged to the room. I snapped out of it and smiled back at the girl and nodded.

"Thank you so much."

I left her on that note and headed back up to our room with a bone to pick with two men. It felt like the elevator was moving in slow motion and took an hour to get up to the room. That was an exaggeration, but that was how it felt time was moving.

When I walked through the door, I heard Julian and Miles talking, but I didn't pay attention to what either of them were saying. Miles was laying on his stomach on the bed and Julian was sitting on the floor. Both of them were facing the TV, watching some sports channel, but that was all I took in before I opened my mouth.

"Why did you pay for it?"

I looked directly at Miles. The room was under his name, so I wasn't sure Julian even had the authority to charge it to a room that wasn't in his name. It also had Miles' card linked to it, not Julian's.

Miles stared at me for a second. "Because I can?"

"Don't bother arguing with either of us, Raegan," Julian said from where he was sitting. "We told you that you deserved to be pampered. The least we could do was pay for it."

Miles cleared his throat. "You mean, me pay for it."

Julian cut his eyes at him. "The only reason you paid was because your card was already on file and mine wasn't."

I looked back and forth between them as they argued about who should have paid and who actually did. Lifting my hands up, I clapped them loudly, gaining their attention.

"You two are exhausting. I don't care who paid for it, but I will pay you back."

Miles shook his head. "You most certainly will not."

"This is where you smile and say thank you, sweetheart," Julian offered as he rose to his feet. "You must be hungry and we've been waiting for you to go get dinner. Get changed and we'll head down to one of the restaurants."

My gaze collided with his and I stood firmly in

place. Julian shook his head in warning and my shoulders sagged as I let out an exasperated sigh. There was no sense in arguing with either of them. All I was doing was fighting a losing battle.

"Fine." I turned to look at Miles. "Thank you, Miles."

He smiled brightly and lifted off the bed. "It was my pleasure. Did you enjoy it?"

"I did," I smiled back at him before moving deeper into the room to find my bag. Reaching inside, I pulled out a fresh outfit and slipped into the bathroom to change. I opted for another sweater and a pair of leggings. I had already showered after getting my massage, but I hadn't washed my hair. I looked in the mirror. It was pulled back in a ponytail and I released it, letting the soft waves fall down the middle of my back.

Sliding my fingers through my hair, I pulled half of it back and secured it with my hair tie. I fixed the mascara I had applied earlier and left it at that. Miles and Julian were waiting for me and as I joined them, the three of us headed downstairs to one of the restaurants to eat.

As we waited for a table, I wandered over to the window and looked out at the snow-covered mountains. It had since stopped snowing, but there was no sense in us heading home now. Even though it was a short drive, it was getting later in the evening—and colder. That would only make for worse road conditions. If they had cleared off the snow, there was still a chance ice could form.

It was safer to stay here.

Even if there was a part of me that wanted to go home. But that came from a place of fear. I may have been safe from the elements staying here, but I wasn't safe from Miles and Julian. There was no escaping them... and I wasn't sure I wanted to.

"Penny for your thoughts?" Miles questioned me as he stepped up behind me. He was so close, I could feel his breath on my neck. I could feel his warmth radiating against my back. His scent penetrated my senses. It took me a second to collect myself as my mind swam.

I slowly turned around to face him, but he didn't take a step back. I tipped my head back to look up at him. His blue eyes were bright, yet they were also filled with a haze of lust as he tucked his hands in his front pockets—almost as if it were in an effort not to touch me.

"I was just thinking about the snow and the roads."

He tilted his head to the side. "Are you trying to figure out an escape plan?"

My eyebrows pulled together. "No." I shook my head at him, the lie tasting bitter on my tongue. The thought had crossed my mind but I didn't think it was that obvious, though maybe it was. "Why would you say that?"

"Just curious," he said with simplicity, but there was something lingering beyond his words. His expression was unreadable for a moment before a playful smirk formed on his lips. "I wasn't sure if you were going to try to run since you're stuck with us again tonight."

"Oh, what a shame," I told him, rolling my eyes with sarcasm heavy in my tone. My stomach fluttered, but I ignored the warm feeling in the pit of it. "That's exactly why I need some kind of an escape plan."

Julian called out to us as our table was ready. Miles didn't step away at first and shook his head at me. "There's no escaping either of us, sweets. If you decide to run, we'll follow."

CHAPTER ELEVEN

The three of us were seated at one of the back tables together. It was a round table, with Julian and Miles on either side of me. We all ordered some cocktails and I was grateful for that. I needed something to loosen me up a bit since the massage wasn't seeming to have any lasting effects. It was like it never even happened earlier today. Something about having both of them at such close proximity now made the room feel like it was closing in on me.

I couldn't think straight.

"I feel like I owe you an apology, Raegan," Miles said softly as he turned to face me. I caught Julian's hard gaze as he stared at his best friend, but there was also a hint of curiosity in his features. "We kind of sprung this all on you and I feel like I crossed a line I shouldn't have."

I looked back and forth between them. "What do you mean?"

Julian stayed silent.

"I can't help but feel like this has made you uncomfortable."

Shit. I swallowed roughly. I was convinced I was the only one who felt it, but I wasn't. "I don't know how I'm supposed to act around either of you," I admitted. "That's why I feel uncomfortable. Not because of either of you, but of my own fears."

Julian studied me. "What are you afraid of, sweetheart?"

This was not how dinner was supposed to go. This wasn't supposed to be me dumping my feelings on the table for the two of them to analyze.

"Losing both of you."

Miles leaned across the table. "So, you're not uncomfortable because of what we've said or proposed? Not because either of us kissed you or admitted we both want you."

I would never call Miles insecure, but his moment of vulnerability was tugging at the strings of my heart. This whole time I was worried about my own fears and feelings of the situation. I never once paused to think about how either of them were feeling or what they might be thinking.

I shook my head at him. "No, that's not it at all. I mean, everything that has happened has changed things between us all, which is what makes me uncomfortable. I don't know how to act or what I'm supposed to say. I'm afraid to act because, what happens if this all blows up in our faces?"

"Would you like to pretend none of this ever happened?"

My gaze landed on Julian's as his voice trailed off. "No. I wouldn't."

"Just be yourself, Raegan. You don't have to be anyone different. You don't have to act any differently." He paused for a moment, taking a sip of his bourbon before setting it down on the table. "Sure, it changes things, but it can be a good thing."

"You're not worried about anything?"

Julian's eyes were fixed on mine. "Why would I be? Life is constantly shifting, sweetheart. We just have to shift with it."

"I suppose you're right," I agreed with him after mulling over his words for a few moments. He was right. Life was a series of events and changes. Either you move with it or you get left behind. And I wasn't going to be left behind. I sat on the sidelines for far too long, immersing myself in my work. I hadn't even thought about any of that since I'd been away with Miles and Julian.

"He is," Miles said with a wink. Our server arrived at our table with our food and we all began to dig in. Miles paused before he took a bite. "I think we're all used to Julian always being right by now."

Julian rolled his eyes at Miles as he swallowed the food in his mouth. "I'm not always right."

"Oh, I know. You just think you are."

I laughed at their banter, shaking my head as a memory slipped into my mind. "You two are ridiculous. But you're right, Miles." I glanced at Julian who raised an eyebrow at me. I shrugged and gave him an innocent smile. "Don't look at me like that. You don't remember that time you told me that the moon doesn't experience moonquakes."

"That was a mistake," he interjected. "I was misinformed and that was the one time in my life I didn't fact-check."

"I don't believe that," Miles laughed.

Julian stared at him. "You were the one who misinformed me."

"That was your first mistake. You should have known better," I said with a laugh before lifting another forkful of salad to my lips. "Miles is just here for the vibes."

Miles looked at me with a facade of pain. "You wound me, Raegan Thompson." His eyes dropped down to my lips and I swallowed the food in my mouth. Time was suspended as he shifted toward me, leaning closer. He lifted his hand to the side of my jaw, lightly caressing it as he pressed his thumb against my bottom lip.

My breath caught in my throat and my eyes widened as I stared back at him. Miles' gaze was still trained on my lips. He slowly dragged the pad of his thumb along my lips before releasing me. I missed his warmth the instant he pulled his hand away from my face.

He popped his thumb into his mouth, his gaze colliding with mine as he licked his finger. "You had a little bit of sauce on your lip."

A ragged breath escaped me. "Thank you," I murmured breathlessly, feeling the warmth in the pit of my stomach while heat simultaneously crept up my neck and spread across my cheeks.

Julian was sitting back in his seat, watching the two of us with a fire blazing in his dark orbs. He slowly sipped his whiskey, not saying anything. Just watching. Something about the entire moment had me clenching my thighs together.

To anyone watching us, it may not have looked as intimate as it really was. It was a fleeting moment, but I hung on to the feeling of Miles' hand on my skin. His thumb brushing my lip. Dammit. I shifted my weight in my seat and Julian smiled against the rim of his glass.

They both knew exactly what they were doing.

And I was easily putty in their hands.

"So, Raegan," Julian broke through the silence as he sat up. "Since this is our last night together, Miles and I were talking about doing what we used to do."

I raised an eyebrow at him, not fully following. "Meaning what? There's a lot of things we used to do."

"Yeah, but it was tradition. You don't remember it?"

I scowled. "We're not in high school or college anymore. I haven't played any drinking games in so long."

Miles smiled. "Only more reason why we should."

I looked between them. Miles was smiling brightly, waiting for my answer. Julian was silent as he studied me with an expectant look on his face. We used to do this whenever we would all get together. We would do an every-man-for-himself and play drinking games. The winner got to pick what the losers did. Usually it was some stupid immature prank and a lot of the time, we were too drunk by the end of the games to follow through.

The last time the three of us were together like this where we took part in our drinking game tradition felt like a lifetime ago. And with the way they were looking at me right now, I knew I couldn't say no.

"Okay."

The corners of Julian's mouth twitched and Miles' face lit up. "Really?"

"Yep," I nodded as I pushed my nearly empty plate away from me. "Let's do it. It's been a long time since we last did and I don't know the next time we'll get this chance."

Miles clapped his hands together. "It's settled then. Julian, you get the bill. I'm going to see how I can secure some alcohol to take back to our room."

Miles hopped up from the table, clearly feeling the energy right now. I watched as he disappeared in the direction of the bar before I turned back to Julian. "How are we going to play anything? We don't have any cups or balls or anything."

"Shit," he muttered as he sat up straighter in his seat and placed his empty glass on the table. "I don't think either of us thought about that."

I slowly rose to my feet. "Let me see what I can do. They have to have something somewhere that we could use. And since we're kind of stuck here, I don't think anyone is going to say no to letting us borrow some extra cups or something."

Julian smiled up at me from where he sat. "If there's anyone who can charm a stranger, it's you."

His words swiftly rolled through me like a rush of adrenaline. The words were on the tip of my tongue and I decided to let them out instead of holding them in.

"What about a friend?"

He chuckled softly. "I'm already under your charm."

I winked at Julian, still riding on the high of empowerment and how damn confident both of them made me feel before leaving him at the table. I left the restaurant on a mission. I wasn't sure if I would get what we needed, but I wasn't going to come back empty-handed.

CHAPTER TWELVE

Miles and Julian both looked up at me as I tossed the things I collected onto the bed. I didn't come back empty-handed, but I didn't exactly come back with the things we needed. There were twelve white Styrofoam cups, a deck of cards, and a roll of masking tape. Miles laid a bottle of vodka alongside everything else.

"This was the best the two of you could do?" Julian questioned us with an eyebrow raised. He was seated at the end of the bed with his legs hanging over the edge and his feet planted on the floor.

Miles was sitting back against the headboard. He pursed his lips and his nostrils flared. "I don't see you contributing anything."

Julian slid his finger through the hole in the center of the masking tape and lifted it into the air. His eyes met mine. "What's this for?"

"Well, they didn't have any Ping-Pong balls, so I grabbed it in case we wanted to make our own balls," I explained with a sheepish shrug.

Miles snorted before letting out a string of laughter. I stared back at him with a scowl as he stopped laughing. "Wait, that wasn't a joke?" He laughed softly again. "I don't think that would work exactly."

I lifted my hand and gave him the middle finger. He blew me a kiss back in response.

"I don't think any of this shit is going to work," Julian chimed in as he dropped the tape back onto the bed. "Except for the cards, maybe."

"What do you suggest we do then?" I asked as I grabbed the things from the bed and placed them on the small table in the room. There was no way that would have even worked to play beer pong on.

Miles rose to his feet and meandered over to where I was standing. His chest brushed against my arm as he leaned past me, grabbing a bottle of vodka and three of the cups. "There are other drinking games we can play."

Julian turned to sit sideways on the bed and Miles handed a Styrofoam cup to each of us before he took his spot back by the headboard. He motioned for me to come over and patted the mattress between them for me to sit. I walked over and sat down just as Miles was twisting off the cap to the bottle.

He leaned across the bed, filling up half of our cups with the clear liquid. "We're going to play a game none of us have ever played in a long time." He paused for a second as he put the cap back on and set the bottle on the bed. "Never have I ever."

"That's really what you want to play?" I asked him.

"What, are we in high school again?" Julian followed.

Miles looked between us. "Fuck you both. Neither of you had any better ideas, so yes, this is what we're playing."

"Fine," I agreed as Julian grumbled something under his breath. "You go first."

"My pleasure," he said with a smirk. "Never have I ever gone skydiving."

Julian scowled, but he didn't make any remarks. He lifted his Styrofoam cup and took a sip while Miles and I sat there without drinking.

It was Julian's turn. "Never have I ever wrecked my car in the snow."

Miles took a drink with a scowl on his face. It was like they were going back and forth, picking things they knew the other had done. Like they were forcing each other to be the one to drink. It felt like a pissing contest in a way.

It was my turn.

I looked back and forth between them. "Am I missing something here?"

Julian was silent, watching me carefully as Miles tilted his head to the side. "What do you mean?"

"The two of you are purposely saying stupid shit to get the other to drink. Why?"

Julian shrugged with a look of indifference. Miles rolled his eyes. "I don't know. Because we can."

"Well, if we're playing the game, then I want to play too."

"Go ahead, sweetheart," Julian said softly. "It is your turn, after all."

I let out a breath, knowing I was about to be playing with fire. "Never have I ever kissed my best friend."

Miles chuckled. "So, you want to play it like that then?"

I smiled sheepishly and winked as the three of us all took sips of the vodka. The liquid burned my throat as it slid down. It warmed my stomach and my face scrunched up in mild disgust. I hated drinking liquor straight. I wished I had something to chase it with but the only thing we had was water.

"We might as well all drink if we're playing the game."

It was Miles' turn. "Never have I ever had a threesome."

The air suddenly shifted between us all. It was electric. My spine straightened, my breath catching in my throat. I wanted to take a drink just because my mouth had suddenly gone bone dry. Not a single one of us took a drink.

"Interesting," Miles mused out loud with mischief dancing in his eyes.

"Never have I ever said I wouldn't have a three-some," Julian spoke, his voice low and husky.

His eyes moved to Miles who simply stared back at him. Julian's gaze slid to mine and I felt the intensity of Miles' stare on the side of my face as my eyes were trained on Julian's. Neither of them were drinking and they were waiting for me to make a move.

Waiting for me to take a drink, yet the fire burning in Julian's eyes told me he was hoping I wouldn't.

And I didn't.

My palm was sweating as I held my Styrofoam cup in my hand, but I didn't dare bring it to my lips. I never once said I wouldn't have a threesome and the electricity in the air between us all was only becoming more intense.

"I propose a different game," Julian said, speaking slowly as he broke through the tension. "Let's make things interesting. Are you both up for some truth or dare, or are you too afraid?"

Shit.

Truth or dare was a slippery slope. We were already headed in that direction and Julian was the one who just decided to take it a step further.

"How is that a drinking game?" I asked them.

"Anything can be a drinking game if you want it to be," Miles said simply.

Julian was still staring directly at me. He raised an eyebrow as a devious grin played on his lips. "Are you afraid to play, Raegan?"

My brows furrowed and I shook my head at him. "I didn't say that."

"I don't know," he said with starlight twinkling in his eyes. "You seem a little hesitant. I think you might be afraid to see where this goes."

I straightened my shoulders. He was baiting me, challenging me. And I accepted his challenge head-on. "I'm not afraid. I'll even be the first to pick truth or dare."

Julian studied me, not even looking at Miles. "Truth or dare?"

"Truth."

Miles laughed loudly. "Yep, she's definitely afraid."

My nostrils flared and I let out an exasperated sigh. "How does it work with drinking?"

"Who knows, who cares. Drink at your own leisure." He paused while taking a sip of his own vodka. "You owe us a truth, sweets."

I pursed my lips before taking a large gulp. I resisted the urge to cough as I swallowed it down. "Fine. Go ahead."

"How long have you wanted Julian and me?"

Goddamn him.

If I chickened out and didn't answer, they would never let me live it down. I was already backed into a corner, so there was no point in trying to run. They were both staring at me like I was their prey. Even if I tried to evade, even if I tried to run, I wasn't sure I'd get very far.

"Since I was, like, fifteen."

"Damn, that's specific," Miles said while Julian also spoke, "That long?"

I looked back and forth between them, not bothering to answer their questions since I already spoke my truth. I wasn't required to answer anything else they asked for this turn. "Okay, my turn." I paused and turned to look at Miles. "Truth or dare?"

"Dare," he said with a smirk. I wouldn't have expected anything less from him and I couldn't help but smile back.

And then I realized I didn't have a good dare. Everything seemed so juvenile and so immature. We weren't kids anymore. Our truths and our dares had significantly shifted. We were headed down a dangerous road.

We were already too deep into this, there was no turning back now.

"I dare you to kiss me."

CHAPTER THIRTEEN

Miles closed the space between us, his hands finding my waist as he pulled me flush against him. A fire was burning in the depths of his blue irises. Holding on to my waist with one hand, he lifted the other to cup the side of my face. He dragged his fingers along my jaw before hooking one finger under my chin. He tilted my head back.

"This kiss is our first kiss, sweets. That last one didn't count."

I laughed softly just as he pressed his mouth to mine. His lips were soft and tentative as he moved them against my own. He didn't move with hesitation. There was nothing but confidence behind the way he kissed me. And then there was a shift. It was as if it wasn't enough for him. His hands were suddenly in my hair, pulling my head back farther while mine fisted the front of his shirt.

His tongue slid along the seam of my lips and a breath escaped me as I parted them. He tasted like vodka as he deepened the kiss. I held on to him, letting him steal the air from my lungs as his tongue danced with mine. I wanted more. I wanted everything he wanted to give me.

And then he abruptly pulled away, leaving me completely breathless as a smirk pulled on his lips.

Our gazes were locked for a moment. Flames burned brightly in his eyes. My chest rose and fell with every ragged, shallow breath that escaped me. My eyes slowly moved from his to Julian's and all the air in my lungs left me in a rush.

He was watching the two of us with darkness dancing in his own eyes. He stared through me, directly into my soul. I involuntarily shivered as I found myself frozen under his gaze.

"Truth or dare?"

Julian didn't move. It didn't even look like he was breathing. "Dare."

"I dare you to kiss me too."

The corners of his lips twitched but he stayed silent. He didn't mutter a single word as he moved closer to Miles and I. He slid his hand around the back of my neck and pulled me toward him as his mouth claimed mine. He was different than Miles. He was just as I remembered.

His lips were urgent. He didn't coax mine open with his tongue. He simply pushed his tongue past my lips, parting them himself as he deepened the kiss. Julian didn't ask, he took. He took what he wanted, when he wanted it.

And I was more than willing to give him whatever it was he wanted from me.

Julian didn't stop. With one hand around my neck, the other was reaching for the hem of my sweater, pushing it up as his fingers danced across my skin.

"She only gave you one dare, Julian," Miles grumbled from where he was sitting beside us.

Julian broke apart from my lips, just far enough for his eyes to look into mine. "Do you want me to stop, Raegan?"

A ragged breath escaped me and I shook my head.

"Truth or dare?" His lips brushed against mine.

"Dare," I murmured as his fingers traveled farther up my torso, brushing against the underwire of my bra.

He nipped at my bottom lip. "I dare you to let both of us touch you."

"Okay," I breathed, nodding. "Do it. I want you to."

Miles moved closer until he was beside Julian, who was pushing my shirt up. I lifted my arms, letting him strip it away from my body as Miles was reaching behind me to unhook my bra. Cold air rushed across my chest and I was naked from the waist up in front of the two of them.

"Fuck," Julian murmured as his eyes roamed across my flesh.

"You're fucking perfect," Miles said quietly as his

eyes did the same. He reached out to touch me and Julian mimicked his movements as each of them cupped one of my breasts.

Julian slid one hand to the small of my back and began to push me down onto the bed until I was laid out in front of them. He peeled his own shirt from his body before discarding it onto the floor and returning to me.

Miles dropped his mouth down to my breast as he kneaded my flesh within his palm. He pulled my nipple between his lips, his tongue swirling around it, tasting and teasing my skin. A soft moan escaped me as Julian's mouth came down to my neck.

"So sweet," he breathed as he licked and kissed my neck, trailing up to my jaw. "You're ours, sweetheart. We're going to make you feel so fucking good."

My mind felt like it was swimming, drowning, being pulled into the deep depths of their touch. Miles switched breasts, while cupping both in his hands. Julian's lips found mine and he sealed them to my mouth. His tongue slid across my own as his hands roamed across the planes of my flesh. They moved lower and lower, until his fingers were sliding beneath the waistband of my pants.

"Tell us what you want, Raegan," Miles said as he lifted his mouth from my breasts. "What do you want us to do to you?"

I wasn't holding back. I wasn't biting my tongue. He

wanted to know what I wanted and I was going to tell him. I moved my mouth away from Julian's.

"I want you both to make me come."

"How do you want us to do that, sweetheart?" Julian said softly as he began to push my pants down lower. "Do you want me to fuck you? Do you want him to fuck you? Or maybe we can take turns eating you out until you're coming for both of us."

Jesus Christ.

His words—his words had me squirming on the bed beneath his touch.

"We've been dancing around this long enough. I want you to take turns fucking me, right now. Fuck the foreplay. I want both of your cocks."

They both rose from the bed at the same time and suddenly it was a race to see who could get undressed quicker. I quickly pulled my pants and panties off, throwing them onto the floor as Miles and Julian got naked. Gone were any inhibitions. We were all purely running off of lust and need. I surprised myself with the fact that I didn't feel self-conscious under either of their gazes. They both looked at me like I was the most magnificent thing they had ever seen.

And neither of them gave me much time to think about it before they were on me again.

Miles grabbed my waist and flipped me onto my stomach before dragging me to the edge of the bed. Julian climbed onto the mattress as I lifted myself up onto my hands and knees. He knelt in front of me, slowly stroking his cock.

"I'm going to fuck your face while he fucks your pussy."

I could have died on the spot.

Miles was behind me, pressing the tip of his dick against my center before slowly pushing inside me. A moan escaped me, my eyelids fluttering. Julian was in front of me, watching as he continued to stroke himself. Miles was large and I felt myself stretching around him as he began to thrust in and out of me.

"Suck his cock, Raegan," Miles growled as his fingers dug into my hips and he slammed into me.

Julian stared down at me, silently asking for my consent. I licked my lips, nodding as he closed the distance between us. Instinctively, I opened my mouth as he slid his cock inside. He was thick and long but he kept his hand wrapped around the shaft as he began to fuck my face. His hand found the back of my head, holding me in place as he thrust his hips.

They began to move opposite of one another. Miles thrust in while Julian pulled out and then vice versa. They were both fucking me from opposite ends and I couldn't get enough of either of them. Julian's cock down my throat had tears springing to my eyes, but Miles had my legs shaking from the force of his thrusts.

Neither of them stopped. In and out. Long, deep thrusts in and slowly pulling out before thrusting back in again. It was the sweetest torture.

"Switch with me, Julian," Miles growled as he pounded into me again. "Come feel how tight her pussy is."

Abruptly, they both pulled away, leaving me panting and feeling completely empty. They switched places. Miles was in front of me, pressing the tip of his cock against my lips as Julian was behind me, slowly pushing inside.

"Taste yourself on my cock, sweet girl," Miles murmured as he grabbed a fistful of my hair. "You're such a good little slut for us, aren't you?"

I murmured, nodding as he pushed his cock into my mouth. I could taste myself, salty yet sweet, soaking the length of him. Julian stretched me even wider than Miles, filling me to the brim in one swift thrust. I moaned around Miles, and that only had him thrusting harder again.

"So fucking greedy," Julian said breathlessly as he slammed into me. "You love having both of us fuck you at the same time."

Tears were streaming down my face from Miles hitting my gag reflex. He did the same as Julian and wrapped his hand around the shaft to prevent it from happening again. Saliva dripped from the corners of my mouth. He thrust slower into my mouth in an effort to take his time and not be too rough.

Julian's hand slid down to my front, his fingers rolling over my clit as he continued to fuck me. His thrusts were getting harder, more forceful, and he was in as deep as he could be. My legs were shaking, a warmth building in the pit of my stomach. I was so close… so damn close.

"Suck him until he comes, sweetheart. You make him come and I'll let you come."

Miles continued to fuck my face and I sucked harder, pressing my tongue along the vein on the underside of his dick. "I'm so close, Raegan," Miles growled. He thrust harder, faster. "That's it. Ah, I'm going to come."

"Swallow every last drop of him," Julian demanded as he continued to pound into me. His fingers were swift and skilled as he continued to play with my clit.

Miles' grip on my hair tightened and he thrust once more. "Fuck," he groaned as I felt his cum shoot into the back of my throat. I swallowed and kept swallowing and sucking as he continued to slowly thrust into my mouth. I drank every last salty drop of him, just as my own orgasm came crashing through me.

I cried out around his cock in my mouth as Julian rolled his fingers once more. My body split in two. An earthquake tore through me, my body shaking, my legs quaking. My pussy constricted, tightening around Julian.

"Yes, that's it, sweetheart. Come for us." He let out a low moan, pistoning his hips. "I'm gonna come with you."

I was on the pill. We didn't talk about it, but no one

seemed to care. Nothing mattered except the three of us and this moment between us.

"Come all over his cock, Raegan," Miles whispered as he pulled his cock from my mouth and stroked the sides of my face with his fingers.

My orgasm was still racking my entire body as I felt Julian pound into me once more before he was losing himself. He shot his cum deep inside me, filling me to the hilt with his seed. I was riding a high I had never felt before. He continued to rock into me until he was done. Until we were all completely satiated and left in a blissful state.

He slowly pulled out of me, his arms wrapping around my waist as he dragged me up the bed. He didn't stop until the three of us were collapsing onto the mattress with our heads falling onto the pillows. I could barely keep my eyes open, even though I knew I needed to clean myself up. I was a mess with Julian's cum dripping between my legs and the taste of Miles' on my tongue.

It didn't fucking matter.

They both positioned themselves beside me on the bed, sandwiching me in between them as they wrapped their arms around me. I was filled to the top, euphoria spilling over the edges of my cup. I had never felt fuller —or more worshiped—in my entire life.

I was higher than the fucking clouds and I never wanted to come down from this.

I never wanted to come down from them.

CHAPTER FOURTEEN

A beeping sound stirred me awake from my sleep. As I slowly opened my eyes, I tried to move and realized I was trapped. I was trapped between Miles and Julian, both of their arms around my body, holding me close. I was laying facing Julian, my face tucked into his chest. His arm was around my back, his legs tangled with mine. Miles was laying behind me, the front of his body pressed flush against the back of mine. His arm was draped around my waist and his face was buried against the back of my neck.

I shifted between the two of them, attempting to free myself from their grip.

"Mmm, where do you think you're going, sweetheart?" Julian mumbled against my forehead as he tightened his grip around my torso.

"Someone's alarm is going off."

Miles stirred behind me. "Ignore it. Go back to sleep."

"We can't ignore it," I reminded them, attempting to push them both away. "We have to check out this morning, remember?"

"Who cares," Miles grumbled.

Julian didn't say anything, he just held me tighter. Miles finally let out an exasperated groan and released me as he rolled out of bed. The mattress shifted as his weight left and he walked over to whoever's phone it was and silenced the alarm.

"Shit, guys, I take that back," he said quickly. "We must have ignored the alarm the first few times it went off. We have to check out in, like, fifteen minutes."

"Fuck," Julian groaned as he stretched his body against mine. "I was hoping to have another taste of you this morning," he said to me as he pulled away. "I guess that just means our time isn't over after last night."

My mouth went dry.

"What do you mean?" I said softly, my eyes trained on him as he climbed out of the bed. They both left me laying completely naked in the center of the bed. I sat up, taking the sheet with me in an effort to cover myself.

Julian watched me as he dressed, but he didn't offer any words in response. Miles was already moving around the room, getting everyone's stuff together. He was shoving things in our bags and grabbed a change of clothes with fresh underwear and tossed them to me.

"Get dressed, sweets. We have to check out and everyone is waiting for us at Julian's parents' house. There was a text from my mom saying we were supposed to be there by twelve."

"Why so early?" Julian said with a hint of irritation in his voice.

I lowered the sheet after putting on my bra and quickly pulled my shirt over my head. Julian was still staring at me and Miles gave me an occasional glance, but he was too busy trying to get us all out the door.

I looked at Julian. "What did you mean... about our time not being over?"

This question caught Miles' attention and he paused where he was standing as his gaze traveled between the two of us. A smirk pulled on his lips. "You didn't really expect this to be a one-night thing, did you?"

"I—I don't know." I half stumbled over my words. "I wasn't really sure what would happen after last night.

Julian tilted his head to the side. "Surely, you didn't expect us to just go back to the way things were before?"

I stared back at him. "I—I wasn't sure..."

"There's no going back now, sweetheart. We're only getting started with you."

I headed into the bathroom to brush my teeth and when I stared at myself in the mirror, my breath left my lungs in a rush. My lips were still swollen and red from the night before. There were small marks on my neck, from both Miles and Julian. My hair was a tangled mess and I grabbed my brush to try to smooth it.

It was a half-hearted attempt. There was no way to tame any of it, so I settled on a messy bun on the top of my head instead. I didn't have much time to apply any makeup so I just put on a layer of mascara and some foundation to cover the marks on my neck. It was a futile effort. It barely covered them, but it was enough to conceal it a bit.

I quickly brushed my teeth before they entered the bathroom. I caught both of their gazes and left without another word. I wasn't quite sure what to say to them. There wasn't a part of my brain that had expected we would be done after last night, but I also wasn't sure. It wasn't something that had come up until this morning.

And my brain was still trying to process what the hell had happened last night.

They finished up in the bathroom and I was waiting for them as they came out and grabbed their bags. The three of us were silent as we headed to the elevator but as soon as the doors closed, they both turned to me.

"Do you regret what happened last night?" Julian questioned me.

I shook my head and responded without hesitation. "Absolutely not."

"So, what's the problem, sweets?" Miles asked.

My eyes bounced back and forth between them as his words penetrated my brain. There wasn't a problem. I was overreacting because I had just woken up from the best night of my life with my two best friends. Even after everything that had happened between us, I was still hesitant because I was afraid.

"There is no problem. I just woke up a little disoriented. It's still kind of hard for my mind to wrap around everything that has happened." I paused for a moment as we reached the lobby and the elevator dinged. "I suppose I was just surprised things haven't changed from last night."

Julian let out a deep chuckle. "You're ours, Raegan. There's no changing that now."

I was theirs…

I let out a ragged breath. "Okay."

Miles slung his arm over my shoulders and led me out of the elevator. "You know that neither of us are going to let you go now, right?"

"I know," I said softly as he released me and stepped up to the front desk to drop off the key cards.

Julian paused beside me. "If you ever decide you don't want any of this or that you don't want either of us, you are always free to speak your mind. We will never judge you or hold it against you."

I turned to face him. "I won't change my mind, Julian. Not when I know it's always been the two of you for me."

His mouth twitched and he nodded. "Good."

Miles walked back over to me and Julian with a crooked smile on his lips. "Well, are you guys ready to hit the road? We have a family Christmas dinner to get to."

"I think you mean lunch," Julian said with a touch of irritation. "Considering they moved the time up significantly."

I laughed softly as we headed out to the parking lot. "The time change changes nothing with the three of us. Neither of you are leaving today, right?"

They both shook their heads at me. "I'm not sure I'm going back at all," Julian admitted.

"Good," I said with a smile as we reached Julian's car. He held open the door for me. "Then that means we have more time together before we have to go back to reality."

"I have a feeling all of our realities are about to change significantly," Miles concurred as he slid into his seat in the back of the car, giving me the front passenger seat.

I simply smiled at him and offered a wink as I secured myself in my seat. Julian got behind the wheel of the car and turned on the engine. We all fell into a comfortable silence as he pulled his car out of the parking spot and drove through the lot. It had since been cleared from the snowstorm the day before.

And I couldn't help but replay Miles' words in my

head over and over as we headed back to Delmont Ridge.

Our realities are about to change significantly.

I hoped he was right.

Because I wasn't sure I was ready for any of this to be over... not when we had just gotten started.

CHAPTER FIFTEEN

My mother pulled me in for a hug, wrapping her arms around me tightly. "Oh, Raegan. I'm so glad you guys were able to get home safely."

I laughed softly, hugging her back before taking a step away. "The roads were fine today, Mom. We had no issues getting home, but there was no way we would have been able to get anywhere yesterday."

"It's a good thing we stayed at the resort last night," Miles said with a smirk as his gaze collided with mine.

Heat crept up my neck before rapidly spreading across my cheeks as I blushed. I ducked my head, attempting to conceal it as I walked over to my father for a hug. The Fosters greeted Julian, as did Miles' family with him. And then everyone was taking turns, exchanging pleasantries and hugs.

It had been a while since we were all together like

this and it had been quite some time since I last saw Julian's or Miles' parents.

Julian's mom linked her arm through mine and guided me into the kitchen. The boys went off with our fathers, heading into the den to watch football, while the women ended up in the kitchen. It seemed very old-fashioned, but it was their tradition. Almost as if the women got their girl time while the men had their boy time.

It was more of an opportunity and bonding moment for all of us.

And I wasn't mad about it. I didn't mind the space from Miles and Julian. They both had the habit of clouding my mind and after what happened last night, I still felt like I couldn't think straight.

"How have you been, Raegan?" Laura, Julian's mother asked me as she poured each of us a glass of wine and handed them out. Eleanor, Miles' mother, was checking on something in the oven.

I smiled at her, thanking her for the glass of wine. "I've been good. I've been rather busy with work, so this has been a nice refreshing break."

My mother smiled. "I like seeing you like this. I like seeing you happy and not stressed out."

"I like being like this," I said softly, not fully trusting my voice. She had been right about living my life. It was a weird adjustment but since I had been back in Delmont Ridge and with the boys, I hadn't really thought much about work. I hadn't thought much about New York. I was beginning to wonder what I was even really doing.

"Have you considered moving back here?" Eleanor questioned me as she turned back around from the oven. "I've been trying to convince Miles to move back."

I took a sip of my wine and sat at the island as Laura motioned for me to get out of the way. I had planned on helping but she made it clear they didn't need my help. They just wanted my company. And to gossip, of course.

"I've considered it... it's just a scary thought with the life I've built in New York so far." I paused for a moment. "It's not an idea I've completely dismissed. After being back here these past few days, it's looking more and more appealing than I had ever imagined."

"Julian is already in the process of moving back," his mother informed the three of us as she pulled a large ham from the oven and sat it on the counter to be carved.

I stared at her for a moment. "He is?"

"He didn't tell you?" she asked me, tilting her head to the side. "He's in the process of selling his home in Italy and has been looking at houses while he's been home."

I considered her words carefully. Julian had mentioned that he probably wasn't going back to Italy, but I was a bit in shock to hear it confirmed from his mother. He was coming back here while Miles and I were going to be heading back to the East Coast. My heart sank a bit. The thought of leaving him here felt... weird.

"Have you been seeing anyone, Raegan?" Eleanor asked me with a look of curiosity swirling in her blue irises. Her eyes were light, a mirror image of her son's.

I choked on the mouthful of wine I was trying to swallow. My mother's eyebrows scrunched and she gave me a strange look as I coughed and cleared my throat. I sucked in a deep breath and shook my head. "Nope. I've been on a few dates, but haven't really had time for anything serious."

"That's a shame," she said with a touch of sadness. "I know you're still young and very career-oriented, but you're something special. Any guy would be lucky to have you."

If only I could tell her the truth. That her son and his best friend have both already had me—together.

I nodded and smiled. "In due time, I'm sure I will settle down."

"Well, maybe with your new outlook on living your life and experiencing things other than work, perhaps that will change," my mother said quietly.

I looked at her for a moment. "Perhaps."

Julian's father strode into the kitchen with the rest of the men following behind him. "What can we do to help?" he asked his wife as he stepped behind her and pressed a kiss to her lips. "Everyone's getting hungry, so we're here to help."

She laughed gently and motioned to the ham. Miles walked up behind me, placing his hands on my shoulders as he watched everyone moving around us. Julian was leaning against the side of the fridge with his ankles crossed and a bottle of beer dangling from his fingers.

"Come on, sweets," Miles said quietly as our mothers all began taking dishes out to the table while Julian's father began to carve the ham. "Time to eat."

I got out of my seat, my gaze still cemented to Julian's. A devious smirk was on his lips as he pushed away from the fridge. I watched the bottle of beer as he pressed it against his lips and tipped his head back. The liquid slid down his throat and his eyes never once left mine. Instinctively, I clenched my thighs together as warmth swirled in the pit of my stomach.

Miles led me into the dining room and Julian wasn't far behind us. I picked a seat in the middle of the table and each of them sat directly beside me. All the food was spread out along the length of the table and everyone began to slide into the other seats.

We all took turns passing the food around the table as everyone fell into a comfortable conversation, catching up on what had been going on in everyone's lives. I adjusted myself in my seat, pulling my sweater dress farther down my thighs before taking a sip of wine.

Julian was seated to my right while Miles was on my left. Miles' foot brushed against mine and I watched as he picked up his fork with his left hand. My brows pinched together, knowing damn well he was right-handed—and then I felt it. His fingertips were deliberately slow, soft, and gentle as they grazed the bare skin on my thigh.

Julian's left hand was also under the table, slowly pushing the hem of my dress up my thighs. My fork slipped from my hand, clattering onto the plate. A gasp escaped me, half from the surprise of dropping the utensil and the other half from the both of them touching me under the damn table that all of our families were currently sitting at.

Thank God the table cloth was covering my lap and made it practically impossible to see either of their hands.

My mother glanced at me. "Are you okay, Raegan?"

I cleared my throat. Miles chuckled and Julian tightened his grip on my thigh. "Yes, I'm fine. I'm sorry. It slipped out of my hand."

My mother nodded before directing her attention to Julian. His fingers were sliding along the inside of my thigh, followed by Miles'. "Your mother told us you're moving back?"

Julian swallowed a mouthful of food and smiled at her just as his fingers grazed my pussy. "Yes. I actually just received an offer on my home in Italy." His touch paused as he noticed I wasn't wearing any panties. His voice was even, completely unfazed as he slid his finger through the wetness that was practically dripping from me. "I've really been missing it here and I'm able to work from anywhere. I've spent enough time away and I'm just ready to be home."

Miles' fingers brushed past Julian's and slowly circled around my clit. I quickly grabbed my glass of wine and swallowed a large mouthful of the dry liquid. I didn't know how to tell them to stop. I wasn't sure I really wanted them to.

"I've been trying to get Raegan to move back," my mother said with a touch of sadness in her tone. "Maybe you can convince her to move back home too."

Julian slowly slid a finger inside me and my lips parted as a breathy sigh escaped me. He turned his head to look at me, mischief dancing in his midnight eyes as he smirked. "I think I might be able to do that."

"What about you, Miles?" Eleanor chimed in with a curious look. Little did she know, her son was too busy circling his fingers around my clit to be paying attention.

Miles looked up at her. "What about me?"

"Julian's moving home. Raegan seems to be considering it. What about you?"

He smiled and shrugged, lazily rolling his finger over my clit again. I was wriggling in my seat, about to fucking come undone right here at the table while he played with my clit and Julian slowly slid his finger in and out of me.

Abruptly, Miles stopped, slowly moving his hand back to my thigh. His fingers were damp against my skin and I fought the urge to groan in protest. Julian followed his lead and dragged his finger out of me, before giving my thigh a squeeze.

I looked between them.

"I suppose if they both come back, there's no reason why I shouldn't too," Miles said before winking at me. "After all, I'd much rather be here with them than back on the East Coast where there's nothing."

My breath caught in my throat as he absentmindedly stroked the inside of my thigh. Julian released my other leg and I glanced over at him as I felt the absence of his hand on my flesh. He lifted it from under the table and his eyes met mine as he slid his finger around the rim of his beer bottle.

The same finger that was just inside me.

My nostrils flared and I pulled my bottom lip between my teeth, clamping down hard as his gaze held mine and he lifted the glass bottle to his lips. His tongue darted out, licking my taste from the rim before swallowing back some of the liquid.

I was going to melt into a damn puddle at the table. I wanted both of them immediately, except there was one problem.

We were stuck in a house full of our families.

"Raegan, you should probably eat your food before it gets cold," my mother said, breaking through the silence that had settled between the three of us.

Julian smirked. Miles chuckled. And I ducked my head, attempting to hide the blush blossoming across my face as I stared down at my food. I shoveled a forkful into my mouth and tried to pretend that Julian's finger wasn't just inside me and that his best friend wasn't playing with my pussy at the same time.

I never was very good at pretending.

CHAPTER SIXTEEN

"Do you guys want to go into the basement and play pool?" Julian asked Miles and I as we were helping clean up. Julian's mother had served dessert to everyone after dinner and our parents had retired into the den, leaving us to clear off the table and load everything into the dishwasher.

I rinsed off the last plate and handed it to Miles as he set it on the rack inside the dishwasher. Julian was throwing out the soiled paper towels he had used to wipe down the counters.

"I'm down," Miles said with a shrug as he stood upright. He glanced at me. "What about you, sweets?"

I looked at the door that led to the hall. Just down the hallway, I could hear our parents' voices as they laughed and reminisced. There was a part of me that wondered if we were supposed to be with them, but this time was ours now.

The tension in the air was so thick, it was washing over my skin.

"Sure," I said softly as I dried my hands. They led the way and I followed behind as we left the kitchen and headed down to the basement. The space was massive and just as I remembered from when we were younger. As you walked into the main area, there was a bar tucked in the corner, along with a pool table occupying the center of the room. Along the far side of the room was a sitting area, equipped with a sectional couch.

There was a door off to the side that had once led to their theater room. We had spent many snowy nights inside there, watching various movies. It had been quite some time since we were all in there together.

My gaze lingered for a moment on the door while Julian and Miles set up the pool table. I slowly walked over to the table, watching Julian as he set the white ball across from the triangle of other balls. I grabbed a pool stick from the rack on the wall.

"How do the two of you feel about upping the stakes?" Miles asked as he spun the cue chalk around the end of his stick.

Julian raised an eyebrow in question. "I'm interested."

"But you haven't even heard what he's proposing."

Julian glanced at me. "I'm interested," he repeated, his voice lower and thick with lust.

My breathing hitched and I swallowed roughly, my

tongue instinctively darting out to wet my lips as I looked at Miles. "What are the conditions?"

"It's simple," he said quietly as he began to walk around the table. "You call your shot. Ball and pocket. If you make it, you're safe. If you don't, you have to do whatever the other two say."

"Sounds fair," Julian murmured as he took the chalk from Miles and looked at me. "What do you say, sweetheart? Are you in?"

I was at a disadvantage. I was horrible at playing pool.

And they both knew it.

"I'm in."

We started off the game with Julian breaking the balls. We weren't playing in a conventional way. No one was stripes or solids since there were three of us. We were all just selecting random balls that we were able to sink into the nearest pocket. In a way, it was completely unfair, but I didn't care. I knew I was going to lose.

And after Julian and Miles both made their first two shots and I forfeited both of mine, I knew I was really going to lose.

"You only have one forfeit left, sweets," Miles said sweetly as he leaned over the table. "Red solid, left corner," he claimed as he lined up his shot and took it.

I watched the ball coast across the surface of the table. "I'm well aware of that."

"You're going to lose," Julian murmured as he brushed against my back and circled around the table.

He selected a ball, called it and the corner, and made his shot.

It went in effortlessly.

My mouth was dry. "I'm also well aware of that."

"If you want me to just put you on the table and fuck you now, you can say that, sweetheart," Julian growled from where he was standing across the table from me. "We can stop wasting time playing this stupid game."

"Hey," Miles said with hurt in his tone. "You said you wanted to play."

"Well, we're not really playing if everyone's making every single shot or forfeiting them, are we?"

I couldn't stop the laughter as it spilled from my lips. "Do you hear yourself? Jesus, Julian. Throw a full-blown temper tantrum, why don't you?"

"I'm not a patient man, Raegan."

I leveled my gaze with him. "Well, that's unfortunate."

I weighed my options and looked at how the balls were aligned. If I hit the orange striped one properly, I could make it into the right pocket. If I missed, I'd have to do whatever they said. I announced the shot I was taking, ignoring Miles' gaze as his eyes widened.

I took my shot.

And I missed it.

Julian raised an eyebrow. "Well, that's unfortunate," he repeated the same words to me with a devious smirk.

Miles and Julian began to circle around the table, heading directly toward me. I watched Miles as he dropped his pool stick onto the table. Julian's hand was still wrapped around his as he stalked toward me.

"What do I have to do?" I asked them, my voice barely audible.

Miles looked to Julian who nodded. "Do we have your consent, sweets?"

I gulped, turning my back to the table as they both stopped in front of me. "Yes."

"Perfect," Julian murmured as he stepped closer to me. His hands found my waist and he was pushing my sweater dress up to my waist before lifting me up onto the table. The cool air from around us skated across my bare ass. "Such a naughty girl, Raegan. You didn't wear panties because you wanted us both to fuck you, huh?"

"Maybe," I half panted as he splayed his palms along the inside of my thighs. He was slowly parting them while lowering himself to his knees. "What are you doing? I missed my shot, so I'm the one who's supposed to do whatever you both say."

Miles smirked as he climbed onto the table with me. Julian hooked his arms around my thighs, pulling me to the edge as Miles slid one hand around my back while the other slid around the side of my neck. "We both want you to lay back and let us take care of you."

"What if someone hears us?"

Julian slid his tongue along my pussy, drawing a moan from me. He lifted his head, his gaze colliding with mine. "You'd better be quiet unless you want them to."

He buried his face back between my legs. His tongue was ruthless as he lapped at me. Slow and tortuous as he teased me with every lick. My hands were planted on the table in an effort to hold myself up. He moved with precision, licking over me before circling my clit with the tip of his tongue.

"You like that, don't you, Raegan?" Miles murmured as his fingertips dug into my flesh. "Tell me how it feels, sweets."

"So good," I moaned softly as Julian continued to circle my clit. "I don't want him to stop."

"He won't," he promised me as he inched closer. "I love watching you like this. So willing and accepting."

I stared back at him, warmth building in the pit of my stomach as Julian continued to lick my pussy. "Kiss me," I begged him, lifting my arms to link them around the back of his neck. Miles didn't hesitate as I pulled him closer. His mouth crashed into mine. I was surrounded by both of them. Completely and wholly consumed.

Miles' tongue slid along the seam of my mouth while Julian's simultaneously pushed inside me. He licked every fucking inch and had my pussy swollen, dripping with need, as Miles' mouth melted with mine. He drew the air from my lungs, kissing me until I was breathless. There was nothing tender about the way he kissed me. He was taking every last bit I could give him.

Abruptly, I felt Julian move away from me and Miles' mouth left mine as Julian grabbed his arm.

"Switch with me," he said, his voice hoarse. "Come taste her."

Miles broke away from me, the two of them switching positions. My mind was already hazy and it felt like I was floating. Miles settled between my legs, wasting no time as he buried his face in my pussy. He was different. Where Julian was greedy and enjoyed teasing me, Miles had no problem going in for the kill.

He was there for one thing and one thing only. To bring me to a state of ecstasy that would have my body feeling like it was going to implode.

"You're so fucking good," Julian murmured as he cupped my face and stroked my skin with the pads of his thumbs. "So fucking good."

His face dipped down to mine and he nipped at my bottom lip, teasing me. "I want you to taste yourself on my tongue, sweetheart."

A moan escaped me and my body was so close to the edge. "Yes, Julian," I murmured. "Yes."

That was all he needed to hear before his mouth was claiming mine. My lips instantly parted, his tongue sliding against mine as Miles lapped at my clit. I tasted myself on Julian's tongue, on his lips. Salty and sweet. I moaned against him and he groaned while swallowing the sound. I was so close—so fucking close—and Miles showed no signs of stopping.

My fingers gripped Julian's hair, needing him closer.

Miles' fingertips dug into my flesh. My legs began to shake, the volcano inside me erupting. I moaned again into Julian's mouth and he pulled away, just a fraction of an inch to look into my eyes.

"That's it, sweetheart. Come all over his tongue." He growled, his hands gripping my cheeks as my orgasm tore through my body with a devastating force. "Come for us, sweet girl."

My face screwed up, my eyes slamming shut as my body involuntarily rocked on the table. Miles continued to lap at my pussy as I was lost in a euphoric bliss, suspended in time.

"Open your eyes, Raegan. Look at me while you come."

I obeyed. My eyelids lifted and I was lost in the dark abyss of his irises as I relinquished control. I rode the waves of my orgasm until Miles was finally moving away from my throbbing clit. I was breathless, my chest heaving with every breath that escaped me.

"Goddamn, you taste like fucking heaven," Miles breathed as he stood between my legs. "We're nowhere near done with you."

Julian released my face and Miles lifted me from the table. My knees felt like they were going to buckle and I stood shakily between them. My dress was still bunched around my waist. I looked between them both as they had a silent conversation.

"What?"

They both looked at me. It was Miles who spoke

first. "We've already shared you, sweets, but we want to try something else with you."

I tilted my head to the side. "Okay…"

"Come," Julian ordered as he slipped his hand into mine. I blindly followed after him and Miles as they both led me into the theater room. Julian pulled me to a stop and I watched Miles as he pulled down his pants and boxer briefs before taking a seat on one of the theater chairs. "Sit on his cock, sweetheart."

Julian released my hand and walked over to lock the door. I turned to face Miles to find his eyes were already on mine. His hand was wrapped around his cock, lazily stroking it as he waited for me. My pussy was still wet and slick from my orgasm. I walked over to him, straddling his lap as his free hand found my waist. The tip of his cock pressed against me and a moan escaped me as I slowly slid down his length, taking him all in one fluid movement.

"Goddamn, you're so fucking tight," he groaned as both of his hands gripped my waist. "I love how your pussy fits around me perfectly."

I slowly began to move up and down, bouncing on his lap as he filled me to the brim. Miles guided me and began to thrust slowly, meeting me with every movement. "That feels so good," I groaned as I rolled my hips and continued to fuck him.

Julian was behind me. His hands roamed across my back, slowly sliding down to my ass. "Has anyone ever fucked you here before?" he asked as his fingertips brushed between my spread cheeks.

I shuddered under his touch. "No," I replied as a shaky breath escaped me.

"We both want to fuck you at the same time, sweetheart," he murmured as he brushed my hair from my neck and pressed his lips to my skin. "Are you going to let us do that?"

Miles reached between us, his fingers brushing against my clit as I moved on his cock.

"Yes," I breathed. "I want both of you inside me at the same time."

"Good girl," Julian murmured against my skin as Miles stared back at me with a fire burning deeply in his eyes. "It might be uncomfortable at first, but I promise I'll be gentle."

I rolled my hips, grinding against Miles. Julian spit into his palm and wiped his saliva on my ass before probing it with a finger. I couldn't help myself and moaned loudly as he slowly slid his digit inside me. It wasn't the first time someone fingered my ass, but it was different knowing it was Julian and what was coming.

"Just need to get you ready for me, sweetheart," he growled as he began to pump his finger inside me. He slowly inserted another, moving them in and out, stretching me open as he got me ready for him. Miles' cock filled me to the brim and with both of them touching me this way, I felt like I was already about to explode.

Julian slowly pulled his fingers out, replacing them with his cock. The tip pressed against me. He applied pressure on my back, pushing my chest closer to Miles' to give himself better access. I breathed in and out through my nose as the anxiety tore through my body. He was too big, stretching me to a point that I had never felt before.

"Relax, sweet girl," Miles murmured as his skilled fingers rolled over my clit, drawing me from the nervous state I was in. "Let him in. Let us both in."

I swallowed hard, focusing on his fingers against my pussy as I relaxed against Julian. His hands were on my ass, spreading my cheeks wide as he eased inside me. Just the tip was in and it felt as though he was tearing me apart.

Miles gripped the bottom of my chin, dragging my face down to his as his lips crashed into mine and he shoved his tongue into my mouth. I cried out as Julian pressed in farther and pleasure mixed with pain. Miles swallowed my sounds, working his fingers over my clit as his tongue danced with mine in an effort to quiet me.

I relaxed even further, getting into a steady rhythm as Julian fully entered my ass. The pressure was almost unbearable. Feeling both of them inside me threatened to fucking kill me on the spot, but it didn't. Miles waited, his cock still inside me as Julian slowly eased himself in and out of my ass. My body relaxed more, accepting both of them as they filled me completely.

I moaned, rolling my hips as I rocked on Miles' cock. That was all he needed for consent to start moving. I lifted my head, my back arching as his hands slid back down to my ass. His hands replaced Julian's and he spread my cheeks for his best friend to fuck my ass. Julian reached down to my clit, one hand gripping my shoulder while the other played with my pussy.

They were both gentle, taking their time with me and making sure my body was ready and accepting of them. I trusted both of them with my life. I trusted them to take care of me—to not hurt me.

"You good, sweetheart?" Julian panted, his voice strained as he tightened his grip on my waist. He rolled his fingers over my clit again.

I nodded, my voice caught in my throat. Miles stared up at me, his eyes glazed over and lost in pure ecstasy as he thrust his hips. His cock filled me to the hilt, each time feeling deeper than the last as Julian thrust into my ass. They both moved together, sliding in and out of me in tandem.

"Let him hear you, Raegan," Miles growled as his grip tightened on my ass cheeks. "Give him your words. Let him know how good it feels with both of us fucking you at the same time."

I glanced over my shoulder, watching the darkness dancing in Julian's eyes as he stared back at me. Julian's hips bucked as he filled me even more, thrusting deeper into my ass.

"Don't fucking stop. I want you both to fuck me until you fill me with your cum."

Miles chuckled. "We're not going to stop until our cum is spilling from every fucking hole in your body."

Julian's thrusts became harder and Miles moaned loudly as he drilled himself into me, fucking my pussy with such force. It was as if they wanted to tear me to pieces. And I was too gone from the euphoric feelings that rocked through my body to even fucking care. I didn't know what they were doing or what they were saying. All I knew was what I was feeling.

And what I was feeling was everything.

"Fuck, I'm gonna come," Julian groaned, fucking my ass with the same rhythm as Miles slid into my pussy. "Goddammit. Come with me, sweetheart. Come all over his cock while he fills your tight pussy and I fill your ass."

"You want that, sweet girl?" Miles asked, his finger-tips digging into my flesh as he bruised my skin. "You're so fucking wet for us, aren't you? Our little fucking slut."

"Fuck, don't stop," I breathed. My head fell back, my eyes slamming shut as I began to see stars. My orgasm hit me out of nowhere, violently coursing through me like an electrical current.

I cried out, my pussy clenching around Miles' cock, my ass tightening around Julian's. They split me apart.

They didn't stop, thrusting into both of my holes until they were falling off the edge of the cliff with me, filling me with their cum. Unable to support my own weight, I collapsed against Miles' chest as an earthquake decimated my body.

My mind barely registered as Julian pulled out, but I could feel his absence as soon as he was gone. My ass ached, but it was warm with his cum as it dripped out of me. Miles was gentle, slowly pulling out of me as he adjusted me on his lap. I was completely dazed, my mind barely registering what was going on.

Julian was suddenly beside the two of us, softly stroking my hair with his hand. "You were amazing, sweetheart," he murmured as he peppered kisses across my face. "So fucking good for us."

"That was—" I paused, a ragged breath escaping me. "That was like nothing I've ever experienced before in my life."

"Did you like it?" Miles asked me softly.

I nodded as I slowly sat up in his lap and looked between my two best friends. Miles stared at me in amazement, and Julian's eyes, they were completely unreadable, filled with emotions I couldn't dissect.

"I did. Very much."

Julian smiled, reaching out to brush a stray hair from my face. "Good."

"This was only the first time we've taken you at the same time, sweets," Miles said with a smirk. "It most certainly won't be the last."

CHAPTER SEVENTEEN

J ulian had disappeared from the theater room, leaving just Miles and I alone together. His hands were soft as they stroked my bare arms. Julian wasn't gone for long and he returned with a warm, wet washcloth from the bathroom in the basement. He walked over to me, his own clothing back in place, and slowly parted my legs. His touch was gentle and he was quiet as he cleaned me up. I watched him carefully, still riding the high from them both.

My body was sore, but I was still craving their touch. I wanted more of them, but I was completely spent. They had both brought me to a place of pleasure that I had never experienced before. Feeling both of them at the same time was something I had never imagined. It still felt like it was a dream, like I had imagined all of it.

The pleasurable ache I felt between my legs and in

my ass told a different story. It very much happened in real life. I didn't just imagine it.

I had Julian and Miles inside me at the same time.

"Come on, sweetheart," Julian said softly as he pulled me off Miles' lap. He grabbed the bottom hem of my dress and pulled it back down to the center of my thighs. I could already feel both of their cum staining the insides of my legs. "We should probably get back upstairs before anyone comes looking for us."

Miles nodded and I shifted my weight on my feet. He stood up and pulled his pants up, buttoning them as he looked between Julian and I. "Are you all right, Raegan?"

I gave him a lazy smile. "I've never been better, honestly." I paused for a moment. "Although, I'm wishing I would have brought panties or something to wear under my dress right now."

"Give me one minute," Julian said before disappearing from the room again.

I looked over at Miles who was watching me carefully. "Where the hell is he running off to now?"

He shrugged and chuckled. "Who knows." He stepped over to me, wrapping his arms around me. "You took both of us so well, Raegan. You're fucking amazing."

"Have you guys done that before?"

I felt him shake his head against mine. "Never. You're the only one we would ever share with one another, but that's because of how we both feel about you. We have a mutual understanding. We both want you and this is the only way either of us gets to have you."

"And you're both okay with that? This isn't weird for either of you?"

"You're special, Raegan. You're special in your own way and to both of us. There's no jealousy, no competition. It's just the three of us." He pulled away to look down at me. "That's all we want. Just the three of us... together."

Julian appeared back in the room. He held up a clean pair of boxers and shrugged when I raised an eyebrow at him. "It's the best thing I have for you right now. As much as I love the thought of my cum dripping from you, I'm sure my mother would appreciate you not messing up her furniture."

My cheeks blazed as heat spread across my face at the thought. Julian chuckled softly and knelt down by my feet, holding the boxer briefs open for me. I held on to his shoulders as I carefully slid my feet through each of the holes. He pulled them up my thighs and around my waist before releasing me.

I looked at both Miles and Julian, the air buzzing with electricity between the three of us.

"So, what happens now?" Miles asked, his voice tentative as his eyes focused solely on me.

"What do you mean?" I replied as Julian walked over to unlock the door. "What is supposed to happen?"

Miles stared at me for a beat. "I don't want things to go back to how they were before. The distance, the time that passed. I don't want it like that anymore."

I swallowed. "How do you want things to be?"

He took a step toward me, reaching out to cup the side of my face. "I want to be able to fuck you whenever I want. I want to hear the sound of your voice and see you."

"We don't live far apart."

Julian stepped up behind me, wrapping his arms around my waist as he buried his face in my neck. "Are the two of you just going to leave me out of this now?"

"What?" I breathed. "Absolutely not. We will find a way to make it work. I don't want this to be over. Not yet."

"You should both move back here with me."

Miles stared at me. "I will if she will."

I pulled away from them and turned to stare with my eyes wide. "I can't just up and leave everything in New York."

Julian smiled, but it didn't quite reach his eyes. "I know that, sweetheart. It was merely a suggestion." He paused for a second, looking at Miles before turning back to me. "I'm always a phone call or a plane ride away. It isn't ideal, but I will do what I have to if it means I get to see you."

"Thank you, Julian," I said softly as I mulled over his words. He didn't need me to uproot my life for him. He simply just wanted me to fit him in somewhere.

Miles nodded. "Whether I stay on the East Coast or move back here, I feel the same way, Raegan. You call and we'll come."

"Promise?" I asked both of them. It was a little unreasonable, but I needed them to make this commitment with me. It determined how my future would unfold. I had been considering leaving New York and they were the two factors that could really make that happen now.

I didn't want to wait until next year to see them. I didn't want to wait until next month to see them. I didn't want the time or the distance. I wanted the three of us together, just like this.

They both smiled and spoke at the same time. "Promise."

EPILOGUE
SIX MONTHS LATER

As I stood out on the balcony, I glanced over to the right and took in the sight of the mountains. A smile pulled on my lips as I breathed in the fresh air. It was much quieter here than it was back in New York City. I knew this was where I needed to be after I spent last Christmas here. It took me a few months to come to the decision to move back, but I did it of my own accord. Although, there was a bit of influence from the two main forces in my life.

Thankfully, the company I worked for was perfectly fine with me working remotely. I just had to fly back once a month for meetings that had to be held in person.

I had just gotten back to Delmont Ridge two days ago and wasn't close to being done with packing. I chose a condo that was situated about fifteen minutes from my parents' home. It was still within the same town, but I wanted some space to be able to live my own life. Not that they were overbearing or anything, but I had worked hard for my independence in life and it wasn't something I was willing to give up.

Thankfully, Miles and Julian were completely understanding about that as well.

They both greeted me at the airport and drove me into town when I first arrived. Julian never left after last Christmas and was currently having a house built in Opal Peak. For now, he was renting a house with Miles in the heart of Delmont Ridge. He offered for me to move in with them, but I wasn't ready for that. We were still navigating the relationship that was blossoming between the three of us. It was still fresh and new. The last thing I wanted to do was ruin any of it.

It only took Miles two months to move back. The two of us saw each other frequently when we were on the East Coast, but he was unsettled. He wanted to be back in the fresh mountain air, where we all belonged. When Julian offered his home to Miles, he didn't resist like I did. He jumped on the opportunity without a second thought and moved into one of the other bedrooms in the house.

I was the one who was afraid to take the plunge.

Being in love with both of them was a challenge for me. I couldn't help but be afraid of what could possibly happen. What if one of them decided they didn't want me? What if one of them decided they didn't want to share and didn't want there to be an us anymore?

The sliding glass door behind me slowly opened and I didn't turn around as it softly shut. I knew it was them. I had spare keys made for them as soon as I got mine. They were supposed to be coming over this evening. They were a little earlier than expected, but that was okay. Even if we didn't live together, my home was still their home.

With Miles and Julian was exactly where I belonged and where I was supposed to be.

"Hey you," Miles said softly as he stepped up behind me and wrapped his arms around my waist. He was the one who craved human touch more than Julian. It was funny how they contrasted one another, almost like a yin and yang. They contrasted, yet complimented. Neither were overbearing and both of them were always attentive to me.

He pressed his lips to the side of my neck and released me as he took a step away. I turned around to face them and my gaze met Julian's. He stepped closer, his hand cupping the side of my face.

"How's our favorite girl?" he murmured before pressing his lips to mine. It was a sweet, tender kiss and I wanted more. He pulled away, his eyes glimmering from the lingering light of the setting sun. His thumb stroked the side of my face and he took a step away, dropping his hand away from my face.

I wanted to groan in protest, but I didn't reveal all my cards. There would be time for that later... when they both helped me break in my new bed.

I hadn't seen them since I moved back two days ago. They both helped me get everything into my condo and then left to give me some space. I was grateful for it but it was also driving me insane. We were all finally living in the same damn town and I had to spend two nights without them.

"I'm good. Finally got most of my stuff unpacked. How are you both?"

"I'm perfect now," Miles said with his infamous panty-dropping smile. "I've spent the past two days missing this girl who has me all sorts of fucked up, but now I'm good."

"Always with the dramatics, Miles." Julian rolled his eyes before smiling at me. "I'm good. I spent the past two days up in Opal Peak dealing with contractors."

"How is everything going with the house?"

Julian nodded. "It's going well now. Things are back on track and it should be completed in about two months."

"Have you decided if you're coming with us yet?" Miles asked me without a second of hesitation.

When Julian started to build the house, he put the offer on the table for the three of us to live there together. Miles—being Miles—didn't think twice before saying yes. I was the one they were waiting to get an answer from. I was erring on the side of caution. Did I want to give everything up that was my own to take a chance with both of them? Was it worth the risk when it could all potentially blow up in my face?

"I've been thinking about it." That wasn't a lie. It was something I had been thinking a lot about and I knew what I wanted to do. I just wasn't sure if it was the most rational decision.

Julian tilted his head to the side. "What's holding you back, sweetheart?"

"Let us ease your worried mind," Miles offered as he stepped up beside me and wrapped his arm around my lower back.

I swallowed roughly. "I'm afraid that if I move in with you both, everything will go to shit."

"Why would you say that?"

"Because isn't that how things usually go?" I asked them. "This has to be too good to be true. What happens when you both decide you don't want me anymore?"

Miles chuckled and Julian closed the distance between us. "Did you hear that? She seriously thinks we won't want her."

Julian clicked his tongue. "Such a silly girl," he murmured as he wrapped his hand around my neck. It wasn't a tight grip, but he had my attention. "I can promise you that I will never not want you, Raegan."

"We both want you, sweets. Take a chance with us. Let us show you how good things can be," Miles whispered into my ear before nipping at my earlobe.

"What if you grow tired of me? What if you both don't want to share me anymore?"

"That will never fucking happen," Julian growled as he pressed his body flush against mine. His cock was already hard, digging into me through his pants. "Tell me, Miles... do you want to share Raegan with me forever?"

Miles dragged his tongue along the underside of my jaw and a soft moan escaped me. "I want to share her until she doesn't want either of us anymore."

"Doesn't that scare either of you?"

Julian shook his head. "You're worth the risk of heartbreak, sweetheart. Are we worth the same risk to you?"

Miles pulled away from the side of my neck and they were staring back at me. Dark and light. Yin and yang. Two pieces that made up my heart.

I looked back and forth between my two best friends. "Yes. Yes, you are."

"I'm going to ask you one last time, sweets. Are you going to move in with us?"

I let out a breath. "Yes."

"Thank fucking God." Julian let out a sigh of relief. He took a step back, releasing his hand from my throat. "Bring her inside," he told Miles as he walked to the door. "Let's show her just how badly we want to fucking share her."

Miles chuckled softly as Julian slid open the door. His hands skated down to my thighs and he abruptly hoisted me into the air. I let out a gasp, my legs instinctively wrapping around his waist as my arms went around the back of his neck.

"You don't have to be such a caveman about it." I

laughed quietly as he carried me inside. Julian was hot on his heels, following the two of us as Miles carried me into the bedroom.

"You let us be the judge of what we need to be for you," Miles said as he carefully set me down on the bed.

Both men took a step back. Miles stared at me as he pulled his shirt over his head and threw it onto the floor. I watched his hands go to the button of his pants as Julian was taking off his own shirt.

"Strip, Raegan. Be our good little slut and show us where you want our cocks."

Heat was already spreading through my body and I quickly undressed as I watched both of them do the same. Miles and Julian stalked closer to the bed, both of their cocks fucking throbbing. I wanted both of them inside me. It was my favorite thing. Feeling the two of them fucking me at the same time brought me to a height nothing else could ever bring me to.

"Lay down on the bed," I told Julian as he reached for me first. "I want to ride you while he fucks me from behind."

The corners of his lips twitched. "I love the way you think, sweetheart." He moved past me to the head of the bed, rolling onto his back as he laid down. "Crawl to me and get my cock wet first."

"Where's your lube, sweets?" Miles asked me from where he was standing by the bed.

"Top drawer of my nightstand."

Julian's gaze met mine and he crooked a finger. "Fucking crawl."

On my hands and knees, I crawled across the bed to him. My pussy was already aching as I circled my hand around the shaft of his cock and wrapped my lips around the head. His hand fisted my hair, slowly pushing me down his length as I slid him to the back of my throat.

The bed dipped under Miles' weight and his hands were on my body, softly touching me as I continued to suck Julian's cock. One hand snaked around the front of my torso, his fingers brushing over my clit as the other moved to my ass. The lube was cold and I moaned as he pressed a finger inside me. Miles moved until his face was buried between my legs, licking my pussy while I sucked Julian's cock. Miles pumped his fingers in and out, adding another and then a third as he stretched me for himself.

My mind was already in overdrive, my body humming from both of them when Julian abruptly jerked my head up. My lips made a popping sound as his cock slipped from my mouth.

"Enough," he growled. "Come sit on my cock. Let us share you."

Obeying his command, I moved away from Miles' face and he pulled his fingers from my ass. I climbed on top of Julian and slid down the length of his cock. He filled me to the brim and I began to move up and down, working my hips as I fucked him.

His hands were gripping my thighs and I felt Miles press his hand against the small of my back, pushing me forward. He positioned himself behind me, the tip of his cock pressing against my ass before slowly pushing into me. I cried out as they both filled me completely.

Julian lifted his hands to my face. "You're such a good girl. Our good girl," he murmured, stroking the sides of my face as he took over and began to lift his hips to fuck me. Miles was behind me, fucking me slowly, both of them moving in tandem. "You see what you do to us?"

"Be ours, Raegan," Miles breathed from behind me as he wrapped one hand around my hair while the other gripped my ass cheek. "Say it. Say you're ours."

I let out a cry as Julian dropped one hand to my clit and began to roll his thumb over the sensitive flesh. "Yes, God, yes." I moaned loudly, feeling completely consumed by them. "I'm yours. Both of yours."

"Always?" Julian growled as he thrust into me harder. Miles took the hint and they both began to fuck me with no mercy.

"Always," I breathed. "I belong to both of you."

Miles nipped at the back of my neck. "That's our girl."

They both fucked me until we were all coming undone at the seams. They fucked me until I had nothing left to give. Until they both had every last piece of me.

"You're ours, forever," Julian breathed into me as we all began to drift into one another.

Miles and Julian had both branded me, leaving their marks of permanency on my soul. Taking me to a place I never wanted to leave… and I didn't have to.

They belonged to me, just as much as I belonged to them.

ALSO BY CALI MELLE

WYNCOTE WOLVES SERIES

Cross Checked Hearts

Deflected Hearts

Playing Offsides

The Faceoff

The Goalie Who Stole Christmas

Splintered Ice

Coast to Coast

Off-Ice Collision

ORCHID CITY SERIES

Meet Me in the Penalty Box

The Tides Between Us

Written in Ice

STANDALONES

The Lie of Us

ABOUT THE AUTHOR

Cali Melle is a USA Today Bestselling Author who writes sports romance that will pull at your heartstrings. You can always expect her stories to come fully equipped with heartthrobs and a happy ending, along with some steamy scenes.

In her free time, Cali can usually be found living in a magical, fantasy world with the newest book or fanfic she's reading or freezing at the ice rink while she watches her kid play hockey.

Made in United States
Troutdale, OR
11/30/2023